AF426980

Also by Jerry Belitch

Population: One
Fifty Ways to Slay

to my parents, Judi and Michael,
nothing I've ever done, or will ever do, would be possible without you

NO OFFENSE

by Jerry Belitch

<u>**Prologue**</u>

MOST TEENAGE GIRLS DON'T usually expect to run into their country's president during an excursion as mundane and trivial as shopping, but for sixteen-year-old Olivia, that's exactly what happened.

Olivia didn't have a job. As a junior in high school, her parents insisted academia should be her primary concern, so weekends were her domain and time she used to do as she pleased. It started out as a Saturday like any other - doing homework, lounging around at home, and texting her friends to catch up on the week's gossip. When an upcoming birthday party was mentioned for one of the popular girls in the midst of her text conversation, Olivia remembered she had a fifty-dollar bill her grandmother had given to her for her own birthday several months back and immediately became intent on spending it.

She made plans to meet those she was talking to at the local outdoor shopping plaza, told her mother she was going out for a bit with some friends, and rushed out the door. And so it was that the teenager found herself just mere feet away from the President of the United States a half-hour later.

What does a person say when they just happen to run into one of the most powerful and well-known figures on the entire planet? Olivia was admittedly at a loss for words and didn't want to sound too overly eager or inarticulate, but her mouth ran ahead of her brain and the conversation began with her declaring:

"OMG! You're the president!" *Smooth,* she thought to herself. *Real smooth.*

The Secret Service agents accompanying the president on his own afternoon travels were quick to act overly protective, jumping in front of him and putting their arms up should the little girl end up being some sort of threat. The president, always ready to bathe in what he considered adulation, was more than happy to indulge the young lady before him, and gestured for his lackeys to stand down.

"Why, yes, I am! And to whom do I have the pleasure of speaking?"

"My name's Olivia."

"Well, hello, Olivia! Always nice to meet a fan!" Wanting to confirm for himself and the sake of his own ego, he pressed her, "You are a fan, aren't you?"

"Are you kidding?" she replied. "You're like, the leader of the whole world! I can't believe I just randomly ran into you! I don't usually get to meet celebrities like this."

"Not the whole world, honey," he laughed. "Just this great, big, beautiful U.S. of A. But hey, you never know. Maybe some day."

Olivia didn't want to leave the scene without being able to visually document this event. "Pics or it didn't happen" was generally the rule of thumb among her peers, and this had definitely happened, so "pic" it was going to be. But she knew better than to just whip out her phone and start taking a selfie without permission.

"Would you mind taking a photo of the two of us?" she asked one of the Secret Service agents. "I would love to be able to show my family and friends."

No Offense

The agent silently relayed the question to his boss, looking at him with a skeptical expression as if to indicate it wasn't a good idea.

"Why not? Just one of the many burdens of being a public figure. And besides," the president said while pointing to his young fan, "who can say 'no' to that face?"

Embracing his new temporary position as unofficial photographer, the agent sighed and gestured for Olivia to hand him her phone. The girl did so excitedly and stood smiling next to her new celebrity friend, while the agent reluctantly framed her and his boss as best be could on the device and snapped the picture. Olivia made to reach for her phone when the president unexpectedly decided to suggest a twofer.

"Let's take one more, just for kicks," he said.

"Um, okay," Olivia replied, thinking the suggestion a bit odd but not about to take the situation for granted.

She got next to him once again for the second picture and tried not to cringe as she felt his hand caress the small of her back and make its way down toward her ass. *Stay cool,* she said to her self. *This isn't just an older man perving on you, it's the freaking President of the United States! Nobody would believe you. He was gracious enough to stop and chat with you, so just take a deep breath and let it be.*

The other Secret Service agent behind them, meanwhile, noticed where his boss's hand was headed, lifted up his sunglasses to confirm he was really seeing what he was seeing, and rolled his eyes; perhaps a bit surprised, but not quite shocked. After all, this was a man with a particular background. But hey, the voters had spoken, so who was he to judge?

"Okay, I think I got it," the agent-turned-photographer said, handing the girl back her phone.

"Thank you so much," said Olivia, still a bit inwardly disgusted with the recent butt-grabbing, but pleased with the overall experience nonetheless.

"My pleasure. I hope those turned out okay. I'm no gadget guru."

Olivia looked down at the phone and scrolled through her gallery, looking at the pictures to confirm their quality. Satisfied they came out to her liking, she pocketed the phone and turned back to the president.

"Thank you again, sir! I still can't believe I got to meet you! My father practically salivates at every word you say."

"Is that so?" he asked, beaming. "He sounds like a wise man."

"He's okay. You know, you're typical middle-class type of dude."

"My favorite kind. Now you make sure to post those pictures online, okay? And don't forget to tag me. I'd like to be able to access them as well."

"I sure will! Nice meeting you!"

"Likewise."

The butt-grabbing incident already forgotten, Olivia went skipping away back toward the direction she came, eyes peeled for her friends so she could brag about why she was late meeting them. The president smiled to himself as he watched his young fan leave, content with notching yet another good deed on his belt, and he too began heading back toward the direction he came. It was like Forrest Gump once said, life was like a box of...chunkets? Chuggets? Nuggets? It didn't matter. The point was life was something all right, and for as long as he held the title of POTUS, he was pleased to be included in the contents of whatever the box contained.

<u>**Chapter 1**</u>

NICK NULLANEY WAS A man wearing many hats. There wasn't much choice. When you worked for one of the most historic White House administrations in recent memory and the turn over rate was only slightly less than that of a fast food restaurant, you had to work double, triple, sometimes even quadruple duty to make up for the lack of overall staff. But hey, he got to occasionally be on television, and his name was even mentioned a time or two. All in all, he had no complaints.

Okay, that wasn't true. He had one complaint. A minor one perhaps, in the grand scheme of things, but it was something that definitely bothered him. The president didn't seem to take him seriously. No matter what he said, no matter what issue he tried bringing to the man's attention, everything seemed to fall on deaf ears. Especially irksome was the fact Nullaney held two different titles in the administration, Chief of Staff and Director of the Office of Management and Budget. This meant the president ignored him twice as often and twice as intentionally.

He knew he didn't always have the best ideas or solutions for any particular issue. Hell, he didn't even trust himself to say anything sensible most of the time. Politics was a dirty game and to maintain the illusion of getting things done, sometimes things had to be swept under the rug. Nullaney knew this, even accepted it as fact, and embraced it from day one of deciding to pursue a career in public service - but that didn't mean he liked being ignored. Actually, forget ignored. Being ignored would be fantastic! For one to be ignored, one must first be acknowledged to exist, and his boss wouldn't even bother to do that much! Why was it he had so readily agreed to work for this man-child again? Oh, yeah. Because the alternative was having a woman run the free world. No fucking thanks.

Regardless of everything, he was determined today would be the day. Today, he would hold an actual conversation with the president, present a clear solution to a problem backed by facts and solid evidence, and be heard, listened to, and - dare he wish it - thanked for his time and effort!

Nullaney had the habit of cornering the president at the most inconvenient of times. It seemed there was always something that required his boss's attention. Fox News was a twenty-four hour cable network, after all. So he had decided to position himself directly behind the big man's desk in the Oval Office with the papers he wanted to discuss spread out all over the place. No way would he be denied this time!

After everything was placed just so, he made himself comfortable and settled into the cushiony chair. He noticed the clock on the wall and realized it was two o'clock in the afternoon. Not that that meant anything, really. What purpose did the concept of time serve when you did the same thing day in and day out? And in Nullaney's case, that wasn't much. Still, nobody had heard or seen from Mr. Cheerful the last few hours, and it was anyone's guess when he would return. Whiling away the time, he decided to take one of the papers from the desk he considered the least important and make a paper airplane. He was a major paper airplane enthusiast when he was a kid, and he quickly got lost in his imaginary world of make-believe, pretending he was a jet fighter pilot and the fate of the battle was up to him.

That's when Boss Man decided to make his presence known and entered the room, furious at one of his minions for sitting where only he himself deserved to sit.

"What do you want and what are you doing behind my desk?" he roared.

Nullaney quickly tossed the paper airplane to the side and shot up out of the chair.

"Forgive me, sir. I heard you were out and I figured waiting for you here was my best chance at us getting to talk. And we really do need to talk."

The president rolled his eyes in disgust, plopped himself down in the now-vacant chair, and brushed all the papers aside his Chief of Staff/Director of Whatever/Orchestrator of Who-In-Hell-Gives-A-Flying-Fuck took the time to meticulously lay out on the desk in discussion order.

"Wait a minute!" Nullaney shouted. "Those are the papers we need to talk about!"

The president again rolled his eyes, this time accompanied by a sigh and a deep breath, signaling frustration.

"You say the word 'papers' and I'm already bored! Can't you for once come to me with a topic of some interest?"

"Actually, sir, those papers you just brushed aside are of very important interest."

"I meant of interest to me," the president replied, glaring at Nullaney as if he should have known better.

This was it, the moment of truth. Nullaney was either going to allow himself to be bullied away yet again, or he was going to stand his ground and bring a serious matter to the president's attention. The nation's spending-to-debt ratio was out of control and nobody had made mention of it for three years. Three years, damn it! As a pledged conservative, Nullaney was many things - a denier of reality, an enabler of horrendous ideas, a mediocre lover - but he couldn't just shrug his shoulders when it came to the financial burden of the future generation. He had kids! Not willingly, but even so. Didn't he have a responsibility to ensure those kids became adults in a prosperous economy where anything was possible?

Didn't they all owe that to their constituents? Or, at the very least, to the multimillion-dollar corporations with whom they conducted business?

"I'm sorry, sir, but this needs to be said. You're halfway through your first term and you haven't once bothered to propose any kind of solution to the nation's debt crisis!"

The president looked aghast and became defiant.

"That's not true! What about that day I signed an executive order of some sort to extend the debt ceiling so we could reopen the government? Everybody thought that was a brilliant move! Everybody!"

Nullaney was impressed. The dialogue was predictable, but his boss was responding to things he said and had yet to kick him out of the room.

"Sir, extending something is just putting off the inevitable. We have a serious problem here that's going to plague future generations if we don't act now!"

The president chose to get comfortable as he leaned back in his chair and put his feet up on the desk.

"Stop being such a drama queen! How bad can things really be?"

"Sir, do you realize, as a nation, we're currently a little over twenty-one trillion dollars in debt?"

The president slightly altered his tune as he took his feet off the desk and now wore the most serious expression Nullaney had seen since their conversation began.

"Well, what do you expect? I walked into a mess here! I've had to undo and roll back laws left and right! And global warming? Jesus Christ, what a joke!"

Nullaney's tone became sympathetic. He liked this man, believed in this man, but something needed to change.

"Listen, you know that as a loyal stooge in your cabinet, whatever you think is right, I think is right. It's just that sometimes I feel a bit guilty when a member of the press asks me your thoughts on any given matter and I have to lie to them rather than answer truthfully."

"Fuck the press!" the president shouted. "It's all fake news! You really think I spend half my day watching TV and planning my next golf trip?"

Nullaney chose to remain silent.

"Besides, most of the crap people want me to worry about isn't even going to be my problem by the time I'm out of office anyway! I wish everyone would quit bugging me with these trivial matters and leave me alone!"

"Sir, while I'm here, there's just one more thing..."

"No! No more things! I'm about to be busy. Out of my office! Now!"

"But what about the papers?" Nullaney cried, gesturing to the waste of dead trees on the floor.

The president decided then that enough was enough, got to his feet, and into Nullaney's face.

"When I tell you to get the fuck out, you get the fuck out! Understand? Don't forget, I gave you not one, but two titles in this administration, Nullaney..."

Actually, I took on the second title voluntarily, Nullaney thought to himself.

"...and I can take either or both of them away, just like that!" the president finished, snapping his fingers to emphasize his point. "Now, go on! Get!"

Nullaney resigned himself to once more being thrown out like yesterday's newspaper and walked slowly to the door as he took a bewildered look around and left. Meanwhile, both Secret Service agents who accompanied the president on his stroll were still on the scene, standing around awkwardly and awaiting orders.

"Do you still need us here, sir?" one of them asked.

The president, seeming to just notice their continued presence, considered shooing them away too, but then thought better of it.

"To be honest, I didn't even realize you guys were still here. But while I've got you hanging on my every command anyway, let me put you two to good use."

"What can we do for you, sir?" the other agent, who up until then had chosen to remain quiet, asked.

"I want any and all information on that Olivia girl we ran into earlier. Is she a student? Does she have a boyfriend? What's her living situation? Inquiring minds want to know."

"Which inquiring minds would those be, sir?"

"Mine!"

The agent who could now add amateur photographer to his resume was the first to show resistance to his boss's request.

"I really don't think that's appropriate, sir."

"And I really don't care what you think!" the president yelled. "Your job is to listen to me without question!"

"Actually, it's to protect you when you're out in public, sir."

The president tilted his head down to the floor in an effort to remain calm. He then went up to both agents, grabbed them by their collars, and pulled them in toward him until they were in his face and could smell every word on his rancid breath.

"Then let's pretend we're back out in public and that girl is a potential threat," he said softly. Then, raising his voice, "Consider it a drill if that helps you justify it, but I want details. NOW! And don't come back without every single thing you can find!"

The agents left the room intent on starting their latest mission, however reluctant they may have been, while the president settled back behind his desk and sat there soaking in the moment. Here he was, the leader of the free world. The odds of his being here were so stacked against him, and yet, he had beaten his opponent. Him! A reality television star, real estate mogul, and, yes, the king (at least in his mind) of New York City! He didn't initially expect to win. Why would he? It was his second bid for the White House when he ran and he wasn't taken seriously before, so why should voters have taken him any more seriously the second time around?

Truth be told, his first reaction to being named president-elect was frustration. He made a good living painting himself as a successful businessman, even if it was more fiction than fact. Why the hell would he want to walk away from that to worry about other people's problems? He didn't! But damn if he didn't know how to appeal to those who considered themselves the Everyman. Turned out he resonated so well with the uneducated, that it didn't matter whose resume made them more qualified for the job. The majority of voters wanted a change to the status quo, a Disrupter in Chief, and when they started attending his rallies and hearing how he spoke to them, they knew they had found their man.

He waited until he was sure his detail was gone before beginning the day's "work," which consisted of scrolling through his phone to check out reactions to his latest tweets, slipping back into his old television persona and pointing around to various areas in the room shouting "You're fired!," and of course, that tried and true method of arbitrarily passing the time, twiddling his thumbs and admiring his nails while wondering exactly how many more hours were left before he could retire to his residence for the night. At some point in the midst of the overwhelming chaos, he felt his eyelids get heavy, leaned back in his chair with his feet up on his desk, and fell asleep.

He was a little boy again, not more than twelve. Alone on the playground during recess, which was par for the course. Apparently, there weren't many kids who wanted to be friends with a self-obsessed egomaniac. He tried to relate to his classmates, he really did. But all of those efforts proved to be in vain. It wasn't his fault he came from a rich family, that he didn't know the meaning of the words "we can't afford this," that his father insisted it was beneath him to take public transportation to school so he was dropped off to campus in a limo every morning. All of these things were beyond his control. People with money usually attracted friends by the dozens, even if they were only looking for favors or to obtain money of their own. Why weren't the other kids attracted to hanging around him? Sure, he might not have had any social skills to speak of, but he could give anybody anything they wanted! Why didn't that mean anything anymore? Oh, well. The burden of loneliness seemed to be his to bare, so he found himself once more sitting on the ground underneath a tree, distracting himself by pretending his fingers were army men shooting at each other and taking down the enemy.

As he was getting into his world of make-believe, he heard a voice.

"Why are you always by yourself?"

The blonde boy looked up, confused. Was somebody actually asking him a question? It turned out, yes, indeed someone was. And not just anybody, but a boy named Vlad. Vlad came from a background similar to his own, so in theory, it made perfect sense the two would become friends, or at least friendly with one another. But they had never said a word to each other before, not even an acknowledgment or nod of the head by way of saying hello. So why was Vlad speaking to him now? Intrigued, he finally responded to the question.

"The other kids don't like me and I'm tired of feeling like I don't belong, so I get as far away from everyone as I can during recess. It's easier to pass the time playing alone."

"You're not as alone as you think," Vlad told him. "Our classmates don't care for me either. They make fun of my accent and the fact that I'm not from here. It's enough to make me miss home."

"What are you doing here anyway?" the blonde boy asked.

"I came to talk to you."

"No, I mean here," Blondie replied, gesturing to their general surroundings. "Why did you come to this country? Nobody seems to want you here."

"I'm not here by choice. My parents thought it would be a good idea to visit another country and 'get some culture' as they called it. But what they sold as 'culture' has so far been nothing but wedgies, people insisting I give them my lunch money, and other forms of bullying."

"You get picked on too?" This took the blonde boy by surprise. He thought he was the only outcast at school.

"Every day."

"Wow, I thought it was just me."

"Sorry to disappoint you."

"Not at all. I'm actually really happy now. Hearing your story has made me feel a lot better." Blonde boy finally stood up and extended his hand to Vlad.

"Hi, my name is..."

"I know who you are," Vlad said as he swatted the blonde boy's hand away.

"You do?" Blondie asked, surprised.

"Of course! We Russians know everything! Well, almost everything. I assume you know who I am, but because I want to maintain the dominant role in this conversation, I will tell you anyway. My name is Vlad."

"Of course I know that! You know, I've always liked that name. It's got a certain...deniability to it. So tell me, why haven't you spoken to me before, Vlad?"

"I wanted to make sure."

"Of what?"

"That we were as similar as I thought."

"I don't understand."

"It's simple, Blondie. You see, I've been watching you closely - paying attention to how you react when the other kids avoid you or say things about you, and how you answer questions when the teacher calls on you."

"You're starting to freak me out, man," the blonde boy said, backing away.

"No, don't leave!" Vlad gestured for Blondie to hear him out. "I'm just saying we have a lot in common and I want us to be friends."

Blondie didn't know what to say.

"You want to be friends with me? Wow. Nobody's ever told me that before."

"You know, it's not just the fact we're both picked on all the time," Vlad continued. "I also happen to know you're a manipulator. You haven't been entirely honest with me, blonde boy."

Blondie looked down, avoiding looking Vlad in the eyes.

"You may see yourself as a victim, but you're really a power-hungry and vengeful kid. I can tell because I am one too."

Blondie looked up again, indicating Vlad had his attention once more.

"We can work together and help each other achieve our goals. We're not going to be stuck at this school forever."

"I hope not," Blondie replied.

"It's true. In time we will graduate, go on to other schools, graduate from those, and grow up to become the powerful men we've always dreamed of."

"Well, I always knew I would be okay. But what about you? Is your dad as rich as mine?"

"Not exactly. Russia standards and United States standards are vastly different. My family and I dress as if we are successful. To an extent, I suppose we are. But regardless, I understand we're much better off than others, so I will be just fine too. In fact, when I get older, I intend to return to Mother Russia and rule my homeland."

"That's co crazy you would say that!" Blondie excitedly blurted out. "I want to run my country some day too!"

"I knew it! See? We are alike, you and I. Destined to be buddies. Let us make a pact, my new friend."

Vlad put his arm around the blonde boy's shoulders.

"Not if, but when we are the great leaders that each of our countries needs, we will always be there for each other to make sure we accomplish our goals, at all costs."

Blondie put his arm around Vlad's shoulders as well before responding, "It's a deal...friend."

The bell rang to indicate recess was over and the two boys walked arm in arm together back toward campus, each smiling with newfound hope for the future.

The Secret Service agents returned to the Oval Office, their task completed, to find the president fast asleep behind his desk. They gave each other a look and just shrugged, silently agreeing the scene in front of them was only too common. Expecting to present their findings to the boss, they now instead found themselves with a decision to make - leave him alone or wake him up?

"You know bothering him when he's napping is risky," the agent/photographer said.

"It's even riskier to not prove to him you did what he ordered," his partner replied.

"True, but this is a man who gets aggravated at the drop of a hat. You really want to be the one to interrupt his shut-eye?"

"I absolutely do not, no. That's why you're going to do it."

"Me?" the agent/photographer exclaimed. "Why me?"

"Because it has to be one of us, and I'm not doing it. I would rather walk away right now and pretend we never saw this and haven't found anything on that chick yet."

"Fuck you! I've got a family!"

"So do I! And I'm a lot more concerned about the well-being of mine than yours, so wake his ass up already, Picture Boy! Tick-Tock!"

Pissed off but not wanting to argue with his partner, who clearly had a better physique than him and would probably win in a fight, he sighed and resolved himself to serving as his boss's human alarm clock.

"Mr. President! We have the information you asked for!" the agent shouted.

The president remained non-responsive, snoring away in his chair, so the agent decided to shout even louder.

"MR. PRESIDENT! WE HAVE THE INFORMATION YOU ASKED FOR!"

That did it. Their fearless leader snapped awake.

"I DON'T KNOW ANY VLAD PUTRID!" the president yelled. The Secret Service agents shared a look among each other.

"What was that about Vlad Putrid, sir?" the more in-shape agent asked.

The president quickly scanned his surroundings, realizing he was still in the Oval and must have fallen asleep.

"Nothing," he replied. "Forget I said anything. You two scared the shit out of me! What do you want?"

"We found the information you wanted on the Olivia chick, sir," the agent/photographer said, approaching the president's desk with a laptop. "These are her social media profiles. You can scroll through these and get an idea of the kind of person she is."

"It's amazing how much of themselves people are willing to post online these days," the buff agent said.

"Terrific!" replied the president, sounding delighted. "Let me focus on these for a few minutes and do a bit of cyber-stalking."

The agents stayed in the room and remained quiet while their Pervert in Chief drooled over Olivia's online profiles. This young lady was quite the Grade A cut, if he did say so himself. Her Instagram and Facebook pages contained photo after photo of her and her friends dressed in various provocative outfits, including several high school girls on the beach posing in teeny tiny bikinis. The president wasn't ashamed to admit he found himself getting hard but his current state of arousal was concealed underneath the desk, so fuck it. Who needed humility?

And then came the bombshell. When he clicked on the "About" tab of his new love interest's Facebook profile, he went from giddy to enraged when he saw she was only sixteen years old. He slammed down the laptop and threw the computer off the desk in frustration.

"What's the matter, sir?" the buff agent asked.

"Oh, nothing at all," the president replied sarcastically. "Just that the young woman I wanted to add to my list of extramarital conquests is a goddamn child! Sixteen years old! A baby, for fuck's sake!"

Neither of the agents knew how to respond.

"I feel like I should be giving you my condolences, sir?" the buff agent asked again.

"You bet your ass!" the president replied. He got up from behind the desk, erection now gone, and walked over to one of the windows, staring outside.

"What the hell is wrong with this world we live in?" the president asked aloud. The Secret Service agents didn't say a word. They knew their boss well enough at this point to know he was talking for the sake of hearing his own voice. Expressing his ideas out loud sometimes helped calm him down when he was angry, and since he had just discovered he wouldn't be able to play Hide the Bone with someone he found himself very attracted to, he was fuming. Knowing his detail was still in the room but wanting his opinion to be known, he continued.

"There was once a time when the prominent, powerful men of society, the ones who contributed the most and were heralded for their achievements, could get anything they wanted. But now it's all about political correctness. We need to walk on egg shells and conform to these parameters built around us or we're suddenly viewed as evil.

"Well, I don't subscribe to that theory. A man should be able to use his dick for playtime on anything or anybody regardless of whether or not society deems them 'old enough to consent.' What does that even mean, anyway? As far as I'm concerned, if a girl's old enough to make a baby, she's old enough to make her own decisions about her love life."

The Secret Service in general had experienced a lot over the last few years working for this man, but this was a first. They couldn't believe what they were hearing.

"What are you saying, sir?" the buff agent asked. Apparently his partner, he of the cell phone snapshot fame, figured he couldn't add anything to this particular conversation.

"I'm saying we need to stop letting people restrict our behaviors! There are so many gay people nowadays, society has let them redefine what it means to be a real man!"

Both agents were once again silent.

"Men need to be men and just grab a bitch by the pussy whenever they damn well please! Someone needs to take the necessary steps to make that happen!"

The president paused as he suddenly had an epiphany.

"Wait a minute. I can make that happen! I'm the fucking President of the United States!"

He fled the room in a hurry, thrilled about the prospect of finally using his presidential authority to do something that actually mattered.

<u>**Chapter 2**</u>

TARA BLANDERS HAD ACCOMPLISHED quite a bit throughout her life, even if she was the only one who thought so. Never one to slack off (though she did enjoy the occasional party and dick when the opportunity presented itself), she had breezed through high school, graduated with a degree in communications from college, and found herself in the public eye at a fairly young age due to both her father's own political career, and now her own.

Politics wasn't necessarily in the cards, it just happened. Her father, governor Tike Yuckabee of Arizona, became the leader of her family's home state when she was a little girl, which put them all on their community's radar for as long as she could remember. Tara found the fame to be a double-edged sword when she was growing up. It was nice to be able to throw her weight around with others and make the obligatory, "You better do this or my Daddy is going to make life hell for your

Daddy," type of claims, but the re-election campaigns and the excessive scrutiny that came with them sometimes proved too much.

She remembered one time when her father, after just recently announcing his intention to seek a second term, started to show extra affection toward her mother. Mrs. Yuckabee thought nothing of her husband's extra attention at first, figuring it was his way of showing appreciation for putting up with everything that being the First Lady of Arizona entailed. As the campaign wore on, however, and Tike's opponent dug up more dirt on him, she soon found out the reason. It turned out her husband had been seeing not one, not two, not even three, but seven women behind her back. SEVEN! How he even found that much time to spend between seven different bedrooms, their own bedroom, and leading the great state of Arizona was anyone's guess. It certainly couldn't be said that Governor Yuckabee didn't keep himself busy!

Needless to say, things didn't go well when Tara's mother found out about all the extra pussy in her father's life. Tara still had vivid recollections of that night. The yelling and screaming, the ensuing fight when everything was brought to light, the denials, the flimsy explanations, and, finally, the decision to remain together and present a united face to the public for their daughter's sake - like anyone cared. The primary reason for their enduring union remained unsaid, of course, and still wasn't acknowledged or spoken of to this day: divorce is expensive, and the more one has to lose, the more expensive it becomes. Plus, Mrs. Yuckabee had grown accustomed to her lifestyle in the governor's mansion and all the perks that came with it. Tike could just fuck right off if he thought for one second she would consider giving any of that up. No way!

That night was the first in her life Tara realized how quickly power could either make or break you. Sure, she understood as a kid her father's connections and decisions could single-handedly help build up a friend's business or destroy that of one of his rivals, but the events of the re-election campaign were huge eye-openers. Tike was practically an unknown before seeking out the governorship, so his first campaign didn't uncover much. That's not to say he was a boy scout, but since he hadn't yet acquired the power he'd later abuse, there was little to no dirt to dig up.

Nobody cared at the time he cheated on a few school exams or that he slept with one of his college professors for a passing grade. When photos of the woman surfaced online, voters generally agreed the professor was hot and if she was offering it, they would take it. Her father's downfall, both personally and professionally, was becoming governor at all, proving all positions of leadership at their core are nothing more than lessons in corruption.

So why did she pick up the baton? Why opt for a career in so-called "public service" when she saw the results firsthand? Because she'd always enjoyed puzzle and strategy games, and damn if the world of politics wasn't the most intriguing and thrilling game of all. Besides, when caught in a corner, she found all she had to do was lie her way out. It was simple, risky, and morally wrong in all sorts of ways, but she loved it! She wasn't perfect, far from it, but she could lie and say she was, and as her current boss taught her, nobody could prove a double negative.

Which brought her to her present-day situation. When she was initially asked about her interest in joining the current presidential administration, her reaction was an immediate, "No, thank you." As a lifelong Republican and fierce defender of her party, the mantra ingrained into her practically since birth was, "Vote red until you're dead." This president was no leader, that much was clear, but she wasn't dead, so on her ballot she voted red. Sometimes things really were black and white. That didn't mean she agreed with the result. This "man of the people" exuded nothing but incompetence from day one, giving major cabinet positions to those who didn't even know such titles existed. Did you want to be Secretary of the Treasury but your wife trusted you so little with the family's finances she never let you touch a single dollar? Done! Congratulations, Secretary Bukin! You want to be Chief of Staff even though the word "manager" is too difficult to pronounce because it's more than a single syllable? Poof! Your wish is granted, Nick Nullaney! On and on it went, with no rhyme or reason for the various appointments throughout the White House, until the president found himself needing to fill perhaps the most important job of all.

"I want you to be my press secretary," came these words over the phone from the man himself.

"That's very generous, sir, but that's a big ask," she replied.

"Nonsense. You'll be great! Your dad is amazing, you're amazing, and I need somebody amazing. So when can you get here?"

"I would really like some time to think about it."

"What's there to think about? You tell the press what I tell you to tell the press and when they ask questions, you ignore them. Easy. Plus," he paused, as if he expected what he said next to be the major selling point. "You'll be on TV."

Tara knew how important television was to the president, so much so the administration was practically run like the set of his former reality show.

"I'm flattered sir, really. But I need to talk this over with my family."

"Your family isn't going to want you to say 'no' to me. Come on. You're smarter than that. I'll just consider this exchange your acceptance of the role. See you in Washington!"

And with that, she suddenly found herself working for the President of the United States. She found upon her arrival to the nation's capitol that her job mostly consisted of making her boss look good and defending him from his hateful and ignorant rhetoric. And, true to his word, most of her speeches or statements were drafted by somebody else, with the content approved nearly word for word by the president. But as she looked over the topic of today's last-minute press conference, even she had to admit she felt uncomfortable. Tara considered herself a woman with a high tolerance level for disgust and content of bad taste, but what she was asked to do mere moments ago was on a whole other level of crude.

She entered the White House press room and took a moment to scan her surroundings. The usual underlings were there: the president's daughter, Yolanda; her husband and self-declared personal aide, confidant, and Middle-East peace negotiator, Ferret Bushner; vice president Spike Vents, and, of course, members of the press. They were all eagerly awaiting the news that was so important to justify a last-minute press conference.

Tara approached the podium, Ferret and Yolanda to her left, and Spike to her right. These people had no idea what she was about to say and she had no idea herself how the announcement would be received. Silently wishing she stood her ground several months back during that first phone call with the president, she sighed, took a deep breath, and began.

"Thank you all for coming. As I'm sure you're aware, this whole thing was kind of put together by the seat of our pants, but the president has come to a decision regarding a new piece of legislation that we couldn't wait to share with you.

"From the start, this administration's had a single goal: to make America great again! We may have our flaws as a nation, but no matter how many times we get pushed down, we stand right back up. Because that's what Americans do: we adapt, we pick up the pieces, and we survive. But we're all only human, and none of us is an island. We need love and compassion from our peers, and we need to be able to reciprocate those feelings, regardless of age, appearance, gender, and size.

"Therefore, in an ongoing effort to promote acceptance and harmony nationwide, the president is pleased to announce the proposal of a new piece of legislation to Congress, the Good to Go Law. This bill will eliminate the age of consent and make legal the romantic pursuit of so-called 'minors,' making love accessible to all."

The room roared to life, abuzz with various voices and reporters yelling to be heard over others in an effort to have their questions acknowledged. On either side of Tara, Spike, Ferret, and Yolanda wore shocked expressions on their faces. Nobody was expecting anything like what they just heard. The only way out was through, so she ignored the noise around her and continued.

"I'm sure you all have plenty of questions, but the president has no desire to comment on the matter at this time, though I can assure you he will tweet about this decision at length as he sees fit. That is all."

Tara picked up her notes and made to leave when a reporter called out a question loud enough for everyone to hear.

"Mrs. Blanders, whether he's meant to or not, the president has been very vocal about his complete disregard for women, as a couple of incidents that were brought up during his campaign a few years ago have shown. Isn't he afraid that by supporting such a law, he'll come across as that much more of a pig and cement himself as a definitive sexual predator?"

Tara glared at the reporter with disdain. This was the part of the job she hated. She didn't sign up to verbally spar with people. Her job was to make a statement, look halfway decent (she would be the first to admit she wasn't pretty), and then hide behind those who encouraged her to give said statements. She was tired and the last thing she wanted to do was make any comments or give any answers that could be taken out of context on the president's behalf.

"I said that is all!" she snapped at the reporter, hoping that would put an end to any further questioning. In fact, just the opposite happened, as somebody else stood up to have her say.

"Mrs. Blanders, can you at least tell us if this has anything to do with the photo of the president and the young girl that's been circulating online?"

A photo circulating online? That was unexpected. For once, she was actually able to give an honest answer.

"I'm afraid I have no idea what you're talking about. Now, if you'll excuse me..."

The noise from those gathered in the room got even louder as people began screaming at the top of their lungs to be heard.

"How can you not know about it? That photo is everywhere!" shouted one.

"Are we to understand the president is making his lustful desires a priority over everything else?" yelled another.

"Does he really think he's going to be able to disguise this sleazy law as an attempt at universal harmony?" cried another still.

"What about all the young girls this law will have a direct impact on? Is he trying to legalize rape?"

Tara couldn't tell where that last one came from but it was hard not to see the concern or logic behind it.

"ENOUGH!" yelled a voice from behind them, as the president himself entered the room. The press predictably went ape shit as their commander in chief appeared before them.

"No one's going to benefit from all of this senseless speculating!" the president berated everyone. "This is exactly why I had Tara address all of you rather than do it myself! All you people do is take things out of context and incorporate your embellishments into your fake news for the sake of making a lousy buck! I don't know about the rest of the American people, but I'm sick of it, and as far as I'm concerned, you should all be ashamed of yourselves! Now, as the lady already said, I have nothing else to add at this time, and this press conference is over!"

The president signaled for his lackeys to follow him and led them out of the room to the White House Solarium, where they could talk privately. Angry, confused, and loud voices faded into the background as the group left the press room behind and settled into chairs in their new surroundings. They all looked at each other, silently asking for the other's permission to address what just happened. Since she was now seen as the unofficial spokesperson behind the event, Tara was the first to speak.

"Mr. President, I have no doubt you mean well, but the next time you spring something on me last minute like that, you're going to need to give me a bit more background rather than just ask me to do you a favor. What's the deal with this photo one of the reporters mentioned?"

The president sat there for a minute, not speaking or acknowledging anybody, before finally deciding to respond.

"I hate having to explain myself! I'm the leader of the free world, damn it!" He took a deep breath to calm himself and continued. "I took a picture with a young fan I ran into earlier today and apparently it went viral. I didn't really think it was that big a deal at the time, but what do I know, right?"

He took out his phone to bring up the picture in question and passed it around. As each person took turns examining the image, there were varying degrees of facial expressions as it dawned on everyone what this picture represented and how the proposal of the new bill came to be. Ferret looked confused, Yolanda had a mixed look of anger and jealousy,

Spike shook his head in shame, and Tara was wide-eyed, wearing her best "you've got to be fucking kidding me" look. Yolanda was the first to speak after her father took back his phone.

"You don't really find this girl attractive, do you, Daddy?" she asked.

"Are you blind?" her father replied. "Not only is she attractive, but during the brief amount of time we spent together, I could tell she's a huge Republican supporter. Believe me."

"Where exactly did you meet this girl, sir?" Tara asked.

"I get bored being cooped up in this place sometimes, you know? Don't get me wrong. It's not bad, but it's nothing like our home back in New York." The president paused, losing his train of thought. "Sorry, what was I talking about?"

"The girl, Mr. President," Ferret piped in. "Where did you meet her?"

"Oh, right. Like I said, I was getting antsy sitting behind my desk all day. There's only so much appearing to be presidential a guy can do, you know? So I had a couple of Secret Service agents accompany me on a stroll through a part of downtown and as crowded as the streets were, this girl comes out of nowhere and asks for a picture. Her enthusiasm was contagious and she was saying how eager she was to go home and brag about having run into me. Really sweet girl."

"I shudder at the thought of being correct here," said Tara, "but this encounter inspired you to conceive of the proposed law because you were hoping to get to know this young lady more...intimately?"

Yolanda shot Tara a dirty look as her father responded.

"Is that really such a bad thing? What's the point of celebrity and hero worship if you can't take advantage of it every now and then? But my hands are tied until this new bill gets signed into law, so I'm doing my best to wait patiently."

"What makes you think the bill will pass?" Ferret asked.

"Don't be so naïve, Ferret," the president chided his son-in-law. "Congress is full of dirty old men just like me, and they enjoy fast-tracking things they know will benefit them."

Vice President Spike Vents, who remained largely silent up to that point, shrugged his shoulders and sighed as if resigned to dismissing the situation entirely and knowing there wasn't much he could do about it, even if he disagreed. So rather than voice any opinion he knew wouldn't be considered valid anyway, he expressed his support in a backhanded gesture before taking leave of the group.

"Sir, if I may," Spike began. "Aside from better serving your primal needs and making it harder for young girls to go about their lives in the face of perverts, I'm not quite sure what your intentions are here or how this is supposed to add to your administration's legacy. But I knew what I was getting myself into back when I agreed to be your running mate in 2016, so if it's all the same to everyone else, I'm just going to go back to doing what a VP does best: nothing. We all know my title here is largely symbolic anyway. But if you need me to do anything that makes you look good, Mr. President, you know where to find me."

Spike got up and left the room, to the dismay of absolutely no one, as Tara continued the conversation.

"So you intend to make it legal for grown men to screw teenage girls?" she shrieked in disgust. "Do you have any idea what kind of a spot that puts me in?"

"What does this have to do with you?" the president asked, clearly confused.

"I'm your press secretary! That means every time you say something stupid or unpopular, I have to make my rounds on all of the political talk shows and convince people you're not some crazy bastard! Which, I might add, is getting harder to do by the day!"

Yolanda had heard enough and rushed to her father's defense.

"I strongly advise you to watch your tone, Mrs. Blanders, unless you want to suddenly find yourself out of a job."

"You can't speak to me that way!" Tara shouted. "You're not even an employee of this administration! You're a nobody!"

"That's not true! I'm the First Daughter! Tell her, Daddy!"

The president didn't feel it was his place to get in between two arguing women, but he hated it when his daughter was upset, so he spoke up on her behalf.

"Well, I am the president, and she is my daughter, so I guess that makes her right."

Tara wasn't buying it.

"Big deal! That goes back to what Spike said earlier! Talk about a symbolic title! God, it's frustrating trying to talk to people who have had silver spoons in their mouths their entire lives!"

"I resent that!" the president cried.

"As do I!" his daughter echoed. "I've eaten from a couple of gold spoons maybe, but I can't stand the color silver! It's so dull and disgusting!"

Tara threw her hands into the air, signaling a gesture of defeat, and stormed out of the room, leaving the president alone with his daughter and son-in-law. Yolanda shared a look with her father and went over to Ferret to sweet-talk her husband.

"Ferret, honey. Could you leave Daddy and I alone for a minute, please? We have some family business to discuss."

"Um, I'm family," Ferret said.

"This is father and daughter business," his wife replied. "I'll catch up with you later."

Ferret, never one to want to miss out on anything, reluctantly agreed to leave and headed back to their residence. Yolanda waited until he was out of sight, then went over to her father and wrapped her arms around him.

"Now tell me, baby," she cooed to the president. "What's with the sudden need for more women in your life? Are your exotic wife and hotter-than-hell daughter not enough for you?"

"Don't call me 'baby,' Yolanda. You're my daughter."

"Well, I did some pretty un-daughterly things to you the other night."

"You certainly did. And I enjoyed every minute of it. But you're getting older. So is Nadia. I need young tail if I'm going to be able to focus on a job as stressful as being president. Did you know they want me to attend 5 a.m. briefings? Like I'm not trying to sleep during that time! I'll tell you, honey, they don't prepare you for this shit when you initially express interest in running for office."

"You're so tense, Daddy. You really need to relax," Yolanda said as she began giving her father a massage.

"It's hard to relax when the media is always trying to paint you as some sort of villain."

"Forget the media and focus instead on your demographic. Your core supporters put you in the White House and they're the ones who will keep you here no matter what you do or don't do."

"I guess that's true," the president perked up as his daughter's words started to make him feel better. "Plus, I've accomplished quite a bit so far, if I do say so myself."

He began to list off what he considered his successes using his fingers.

"I've pissed off foreign leaders, I give science the finger daily, and let's not forget I single-handedly gave Hawaii their statehood. They were just a random island floating out in the middle of nowhere before I declared them a U.S. territory. Everyone was thrilled about that. So many people loved that decision."

"And you're just getting started," Yolanda told him.

"You're right," he chuckled. "You're always right."

He leaned back in his chair, visibly content and more at ease than he was earlier, while his daughter continued his massage.

Chapter 3

"PEOPLE ARE EXPERIENCING MIXED feelings nationwide today over a pending piece of legislation currently being referred to as the Good to Go Law," a news anchor for the Alpha Beta Network said to his viewers. A graphic then appeared on screen showing a pie chart of people surveyed in which the results appeared to be evenly split.

"As you can see," the anchor continued, "it's a pretty even divide. Roughly fifty percent of those surveyed consider the proposed law 'appalling,' with some even going so far as to consider it the equivalent of legalizing rape. The other fifty percent claim they're undecided, waiting to see how the potential passing of the bill will change the overall behavior of their peers before they themselves pass judgment."

The channel was then changed to the Pretty Birdie Network, whose prime-time anchor was also reporting reactions from the day's press conference.

"Polls are being conducted left and right in an effort to find out just how much society really needs this so-called Good to Go Law." Another graphic appeared on screen. "As the graphic to the side of me shows, fifty-four percent of those surveyed claim they'll support anything the president says, even if it means their children end up losing their innocence a little earlier than planned. Forty-four percent hate the idea, claiming it's not only an attack on children, but a complete disregard for common sense and maturity. The remaining two percent are undecided, leading to speculation that this could be a group of asexuals who don't much care about the matter one way or the other."

The person watching television changed the channel yet again to the Biased News network, just to switch things up.

"Clearly our president is a visionary," the BNN anchor said. "I mean, there's no denying all the good he's done over the course of the last few years, but now he presents us with this genius new idea and it's like, of course we should be able to express our love to anybody! Why didn't anyone think of this sooner? Should the law pass, it goes without saying that our commander in chief will go down in history as a true man of the people."

Another channel change.

"...and as the Good to Go Law is expected to make its way to the House of Representatives, the question for those of us who have a conscience is, if it's now going to be legal to fornicate with literally anyone, what will this end up meaning for abortion and a woman's right to choose? Such a debate arising from young ladies being deemed 'good to go' is only a matter of time, and the results could very well end up having far-reaching consequences."

Briana Gifford, a retired porn star formerly known by her stage name, Red Velvet, decided to turn the television off for the night. She had heard all she needed to hear. Frustrated, she lay down on the couch in her living room, trying to wrap her head around the president's latest antics and the fact they were picking up steam. Briana knew all too well what kind of man the president was and couldn't stand the newly proposed legislation.

"Ongoing effort to promote harmony, my ass," she said out loud to herself.

Briana's husband, Dennis, a fellow retired porn star formerly known by his stage name, Mac Daddy, entered the room to see what had his wife so upset.

"Did you say something, baby?" he asked. "Everything all right?"

"I was just talking to myself," his wife replied. "Have you heard about this 'Good to Go' law? The thought of it passing really aggravates me."

"You know I'm not one for gossip," he said as he joined his wife on the couch.

"It's not just gossip when it can impact people's lives, dear."

"Yeah, I guess so. Still, I tend to keep my distance from the outside world."

"Oh, that's right. For a second I forgot what a regular fountain of knowledge you are," Briana teased. "Remind me again why I married you?"

"I'd like to think it's because when we met on set, you saw my horse-sized junk and it made you all tingly inside."

"Yeah, that must have been it," Briana said, rolling her eyes.

"It's still the same size, even after all of these years. You can attest to that. You were playing with it just last night."

"Was I now? Huh. I must have thought it was somebody else's. Or maybe I was just fantasizing it was somebody else's."

"Ha ha. You're hilarious."

"I really am."

The two of them made out for a bit before Briana broke it off and pushed her husband away.

"In all seriousness, honey, just listen to me for a minute. With this law, the president wants to ensure he can continue to be the sexual predator he's always been, but now he wants it to be considered legal."

Dennis sat up straight. His wife had his attention.

"This isn't going to be easy for me, but when it comes to our wonderful Narcissist in Chief, there's something I'm finally ready to tell you."

There were roughly a dozen teenage girls, varying in appearance and age from thirteen to eighteen, sitting in chairs and looking into vanity mirrors as they got their hair and makeup done. The girls chatted among themselves excitedly as they had just been told the annual Pretty Little Miss Pageant they were participating in was going to be locally televised this year. Talk quickly turned to how many of their friends might watch the broadcast when the man who would one day be President of the United States entered the room. Known back then as a business man and real estate mogul, he was also the primary sponsor of the annual pageant that attracted teen girls from all over the country to participate and try their hand at winning the crown. Since the event wouldn't exist without him, he felt entitled to go backstage whenever he pleased and observe the girls in various states of undress. It never struck him as inappropriate that a grown man should have such access to scantily clad young ladies. If anything, he was owed this view of these stunning creatures. Not being able to see exactly where his money was going and what results it produced, that's what would have been inappropriate.

"Ten minutes before showtime, girls," he announced to what he considered his investments. "But don't worry, you all look amazing. I wouldn't kick any of you out of my bed."

He looked around the room, enjoying the view, before his eyes settled on one girl in particular, a seventeen-year-old Briana Gifford.

"How adorable are you!" he said to Briana as he approached her. He found himself eager to have a conversation with this young lady and get to know her a bit, but to his surprise, he was completely ignored.

Briana stared straight ahead, continuing to look into her vanity mirror, pretending the man now uncomfortably close to her wasn't there. She knew what he was about - how his sponsorship dollars of the pageant gave him some sort of misplaced sense of self, how he was always making crude comments to the contestants – and she wasn't having any of it. She knew she was pretty, that's why she was there, but that didn't mean she had to accept or allow this man to degrade her or talk down to her as if she was nothing more than a piece of meat. The only thing she wanted to do today was win this competition and hopefully kick-start a modeling career. She would maybe flirt with a judge or two if it was necessary, but that's as far as she would go. At least, that's what she told herself.

"You know, I have quite a bit of influence around here, since I pay the bills and whatnot," the man tried again. "But I'm sure you already know that."

Yes, she knew it all right, and she wasn't going to let that distract her or result in her doing anything she would regret. Probably.

The future president could tell he wasn't getting anywhere, but a determined man on the prowl, especially one with as many resources as he had, didn't give up that easily. He decided to press forward.

"What if I said I could guarantee you win this thing? Would you acknowledge me then?"

Silence still.

"You're a smart girl. I respect that. But being who I am, I have an offer for you." He reached into his coat pocket for his checkbook, wrote Briana a check for ten thousand dollars, and slapped it down on the dresser next to her. Her eyes went wide when she saw the amount, which finally coaxed her to speak.

"Why would you give this to me? What do you want?"

"Come now, don't be so naïve. I think we both know what I want. Forget about this pageant and leave here with me, now."

"You mean you expect me to...?" She had a feeling this was coming, though she was still surprised by and abrasive to the idea.

"I'm expecting you to prove you're worth the amount written on that check, yes."

"Why me?"

"Well, aside from obviously being the most beautiful girl here, you also strike me as the oldest. And I'm willing to bet that means you've either already done things or are aware of things I would have to explain to the younger girls. As a businessman, you learn that time is money, and I don't want to waste my time teaching when I can just get right down to

doing."

"Sexual things?"

"Drop the act, honey. We've already established that. Now, take a look around you. Out of everyone here, you're the one who landed on my radar. If you want any kind of real future in this business of show, you'll realize my attention means something. So, that leaves us with one final question." He extended his arm out to Briana in a gesture indicating she should hook it around his. "Are you in or out?"

Briana, check in hand, looked back and forth between the despicable man next to her, and the piece of paper that would lead to one hell of a payday. After a few moments of inner turmoil where she briefly struggled with her conscience, she heaved a sigh of defeat, pocketed the check, and allowed her new date for the evening to lead her away.

Ever the classy type, he took her to a cheap motel where the walls were thin, the room reeked of cigarette smoke and urine, and the mattress was just barely functional enough to allow them to do the deed. When it was over, they lay in bed together, each unsure of how to react or what to say. Awkward silence and tension was in the air, with neither one choosing to speak or look at the other. After a while, Briana decided it was time to go and got out of bed to pick up her clothes off the floor and start getting dressed.

"Leaving so soon?" the man finally spoke as he noticed her putting her dress back on.

Briana chose to return to the cold shoulder routine. Having fulfilled her duties and living up to her side of their deal, she had earned her money and there was nothing else to do but leave.

"Come on!" the man pleaded. "After everything we just did, you think you'd at least be able to talk to me!"

Briana, only half-clothed, turned around and gave her lover an angry glare.

"What happened only happened because I could really use the money! Even if you hadn't talked me into coming here with you and I had ended up winning the pageant, whatever I would have received for first place wouldn't have come close to the amount you gave me!"

"Yeah, it's an event with pretty cheap stakes, that's for sure," he chuckled. "Whoever's in charge should do something about that."

Briana rolled her eyes and finished getting dressed.

"Lighten up! I'm kidding! Obviously, we both know I could up the ante a bit if I wanted, but why should I? The invaluable exposure the girls receive should be prize enough. You know how many models working in the fashion industry today got their start from my pageant? Plenty, believe me."

"I don't believe you!" Briana yelled, frustrated. "I can't believe a single word that comes out of your mouth, and I'm surprised that so many people do!"

"It's the art of the deal, baby. It involves carefully worded rhetoric and implanting just enough self-doubt in others to manipulate them into believing anything can happen."

"Where did that come from?" Briana asked, slack-jawed.

"What?"

"That explanation you just gave me. I thought you were an idiot with no vocabulary!"

"True, I'm not the brainiest guy at the science fair, but again, it's all about manipulation. I know exactly what I'm saying and doing at all times, I just don't give a fuck. And don't let anybody tell you differently."

Fully dressed, Briana sat on the edge of the bed, indicating she might be up for some small talk after all.

"Why do I get the feeling you're full of shit and I'm being manipulated as we speak?"

"Because like I said earlier, you're a smart girl. I actually heard someone from my PR firm say that to me one time and it's one of the few things I listened to, so I borrow it every now and then. But enough about me."

He put his hand on Briana's leg before continuing.

"I want to know more about you. This doesn't have to be a one-time thing. We can meet up whenever you'd like. I might even start to grow on you."

"Would you pay me every time?" she asked.

"Maybe not ten grand, but I'd be willing to slip you a few bucks here and there. Or I could give you my number and if you ever needed anything, all you'd have to do is call. A favor with my name has weight on it, no matter what people might say."

Briana gave the offer serious consideration. How else would a girl her age get that kind of money? And favors? This could be her ticket to full-time modeling!

"And it wouldn't bother you you'd be resorting to a seventeen-year-old to get laid?"

An expression of shock immediately came over the man and he went as slack-jawed as his young lover did earlier.

"You're only seventeen?"

"Yeah. Why? You thought I was older?"

"Well, fucking DUH!" he shouted, now in a rush to leave himself and hurriedly getting out of bed to fetch his clothes.

"But you met me at a teenage pageant for girls that YOU run. How old could I possibly be?"

"I thought at least eighteen or nineteen!" he replied. "Anyone with eyes could see you were the most developed girl there, and with that body and the way you carry yourself, I figured you must be legal!"

"Well, you figured wrong."

"Again, fucking DUH!"

Now also fully dressed, the despicable excuse for a man once more reached into his coat pocket and pulled out his checkbook. He quickly scribbled another amount on a new check and handed it to Briana.

"Holy shit!" Briana cried. "Two million dollars?"

"I'm buying your silence. No one hears about this, you understand? Not one person! I'll consider the cashing of that check a verbal agreement. I don't care what you tell people you were up to all night, just as long as you don't mention me. I was never here and I have no idea who you are. Goodbye!"

The man left the motel room and slammed the door shut behind him, leaving an elated Briana by herself, still staring at the check.

Briana sat with tears in her eyes as she finished telling her story to her husband.

"I promised myself I would never tell that story to anyone, especially since I come off just as guilty. I took the money and used it for my own benefit, which makes me no better than some cheap whore."

"On the contrary," Dennis reassured his wife, "You said you made two million, ten thousand dollars that night. That's hardly the income of a cheap whore."

"Stop trying to make me laugh," Briana said, giggling. "I'm pouring my heart out here to prove a point."

"That our president is a sleazeball? Shocker. Sorry, baby, but that's not exactly life-changing news."

"Then why do so many people admire the guy? What the hell is wrong with everybody?"

"Couldn't tell you. I don't care for the outside world, remember?"

Dennis got up to head to the kitchen for a drink while Briana reached for her laptop from the coffee table in front of the couch.

"I'll bet I can finally convince people what kind of man their hero is if I take my story public," she said, Googling some of her old contacts.

Dennis returned with a beer and joined his wife back on the couch.

"Maybe, maybe not. I may not know much about the guy, but I do know that his supporters are so fiercely loyal that if he declared tomorrow National Suicide Day, our surroundings would suddenly be a lot less over-populated."

"You think so?"

"I know so. Look at some of the things he's said and done already."

"I thought you didn't bother tuning into the outside world," Briana chided her husband.

"Whether or not I want to, I still hear things. There's no doubt the guy's a fucking maniac who's in way over his head, but good luck telling the masses that. As far as they're concerned, nothing he does is wrong. It's eerie."

"Well, I've got to try. At the very least, I might be able to hinder this Good to Go Law from passing."

Dennis put his feet up on the coffee table and took a swig of his beer.

"I'm behind you, baby, one hundred percent," he said. "You know that."

"I do know that," she replied. "Thanks."

"Besides, you can't lose here."

"What do you mean?"

"Even if nobody believes you, the public still hears your name again. And if they do believe you, others might be encouraged to come forward. It's a win-win."

"I hadn't thought of that," Briana said, looking thoughtfully into space for a minute. "You think other women might have stories similar to mine?"

"It's a possibility. Unfortunately, people tend to favor celebrity status over damn near everything else, so they look the other way and pretend things like that never happened."

"Not anymore! I've still got some media contacts from our days in the porn industry. I'm going to reach out to them and see if anyone proves to be useful."

Briana became laser-focused on her laptop and began searching through her old contacts for anyone willing to let her talk on the air or in print, hoping to be able to stir the pot and shed some light on what she now believed was the world's worst-kept secret.

Chapter 4

LIFE WAS PRETTY GOOD for television and radio personality, Bryan Seachest. Glorified Karaoke, the number one reality show in America over twenty seasons strong, gave a major boost to his career back in 2000 after he beat out a slew of other pretty boys to land the hosting gig, which resulted in further hosting opportunities that led to a mini media empire of sorts. He became the face of New Year's Eve once people started tuning in for his annual commentary and to watch him drop the symbolic New Year's Ball during his live broadcast every year; he recently received the opportunity to co-host a popular daytime talk show after the show's diva female host stopped getting along with her on-air male counterpart; he started becoming a regular fixture on just about every awards and music show in existence; he began producing his own reality shows earlier this year; and the offers just kept coming.

Some colleagues and friends even suggested he launch his own television network. The thought had crossed his mind before, but he wasn't sure if he had his hands in enough productions to justify such an endeavor. Sure, there were probably a dozen shows that currently carried his name in the credits to some extent, but an entire network where nothing but those same shows were played over and over? That seemed a bit much. He loved attention as much as the next celebrity, but people didn't need to have access to shows like Keeping Up For No Reason or Desperate Quest For Fame on a 24/7 basis, though the latter had inexplicably become just as popular lately, if not more so, than Glorified Karaoke, and he would tell anyone who asked that of all his projects, that one was his favorite.

It was a simple premise: families from all walks of life applied each season to have camera crews follow them around anywhere and everywhere and have various recording devices installed in every room of their home to ensure there wasn't a single second of their lives that went undocumented. A different family was introduced to the world each year and for ten months and roughly two hundred episodes per season, viewers fell head over heels for these people as they learned everything about their personal and professional lives. The best part for him, personally? Aside from the cost of hiring a team to operate the cameras and recording equipment and editing the massive amounts of footage into a coherent episodic narrative, the show was insanely cheap to produce, bringing in hundreds of millions for everyone involved behind the scenes.

Of course, there was always the criticism from those claiming all he did was exploit whatever family was currently being followed around, but fuck the critics! He never asked to turn people's lives into a circus, they always came to him! Besides, they were compensated decently for their time (not great, considering the money the show always brought in, but decently), and they eventually faded into obscurity anyway like all other fads of the moment as soon as the next season with fresh faces began. So all in all, the process was quite harmless. Those starving for it received their fifteen minutes of fame and Seachest and his team took daily swims in their mountains of cash. Everybody benefited.

As much as he liked the world of television, though, radio opened up additional possibilities for advertising revenue and getting his opinions and voice heard in millions of homes on a daily basis. He didn't consider himself much of a radio guy at first, figuring all of his on-camera time was more than enough to push his "brand," whatever that was. But the more he heard about new podcasts and internet radio shows popping up every day, the more he thought, why not me? Thus, the concept for Taking Over with Bryan Seachest was born.

Another daily show to produce was going to seriously cut into his precious mid-afternoon nap time, which he needed with all the traveling he did between sets, but hey, we can all sleep when we're dead, right? So it was that the radio show became yet another all-consuming focus, broadcast every afternoon in syndication around the country. Seachest used the airtime to editorialize on current events, tell anecdotes he thought his fans would just love to hear, interview his celebrity friends, and, since it was radio, play the obligatory music the good old Payola scandals that were still alive and well dictated must be heard, every hour on the hour.

There was a brief moment of drama when he began dating his then-co-host which led to what in hindsight became a way-too-soon engagement announcement, which in turn led to the wedding being called off, which then led to a highly publicized break-up and falling out - but such was life in the public eye. Seachest loved women, which didn't make him a bad person, just human. Likewise, being he was the prototypical pretty boy, women also loved him. This proved several times throughout his career to be a double-edged sword, but one he was willing to take into battle if it meant getting laid regularly, so deal with it he did. The main problem he constantly found was there was too much potential for bed wrestling and not enough hours in the day. Everywhere he looked, there were women he knew would get naked for him just by him walking up to them and saying, "Hi" (and that was usually the only opening line he needed). But there were also the stubborn ones, those who would acknowledge his Hollywood status and looks but would refuse to be taken on a safari. Such was the case with his latest assistant, Erica Sudds.

From the moment she interviewed to work for him, he knew he had to have her. With dark curly hair, a dark skin tone to match (not necessarily black, but a color that indicated she was definitely a mix), and great legs carrying an even better body, he was hard for her almost constantly. He would often resort to making jokes based on sexual innuendos and brush up against her just to have some sort of contact with her skin. It never worked. She never once blushed or swatted him away in a playful or flirtatious manner that suggested she was picking up on his hints or interested in crossing that line in any way. It frustrated the hell out of him.

So one day while they were both in his dressing room waiting to start the next taping of Glorified Karaoke, he blurted it out.

"I'm looking for a new co-host for my radio show."

Erica became a lot more animated around her boss from that moment on, knowing that such a gig would not only come with a significant pay raise, but could also potentially give her the media career she'd always wanted and change her life forever. As he expected, all the flirting and innuendos soon followed, making the consummation of their agreement, one promotion for one sexual affair, an inevitability.

They were currently on the couch in the same dressing room he first seduced her in on that first day, finishing up their most recent tryst. When they were done, Erica grabbed the blanket on top of them and wrapped it around her as she got up and headed to the mini fridge for a bottle of water. Seachest sat up and stayed on the couch, watching her walk to the other side of the room and wondering why he hadn't told her about the co-hosting opportunity sooner. The woman was an amazing lover, and he silently patted himself on the back for finally finding a way into her pants. Once she sat down on a stool with the blanket completely wrapped around her and the bottle of water in hand, he broke the silence hovering over them like a mist.

"That was good, right?" he asked smugly. "Worth the job I promised you?"

"It was okay. My boyfriend's better, but don't take that personally. He knows me so he knows what I like."

"Yeah, well, your boyfriend doesn't have a radio show with a vacant co-hosting seat, does he?"

"No, he sure doesn't. And no offense, Bryan, but I feel it's important I remind you that that's literally the only reason why this happened."

"Come on, Erica. Don't be so coy. You wanted this as much as I did."

"What gives you that idea?"

"Well, I'll admit you were a tough nut to crack, but I saw the way you made eyes at me once I finally got your attention; noticed how you would sprinkle innuendos in your communication with me every time you gave me my schedule for the day; always making a point of being back here with me whenever I was preparing for a shoot. The signs were all there."

Erica couldn't believe what she was hearing. Did this man really believe her affection towards him lately was genuine and not just some play at workplace politics?

"The signs were all there?" she said, anger just beneath the surface of her tone. "First of all, I've never made eyes at you. Not once! I know this because they're my eyes and I don't look at you unless I have to. Not that you're ugly, but your my boss and that wouldn't be right. Second, any 'innuendo' as you called it, was never done as flirtation, only as a joke. Again, you're my boss. But I know you've wanted me since day one, so I let everything you said and did slide, including brushing up against me, because yes, I knew what that was about, how could I not? I ignored it because I need this job, and you know I need this job, which is why I decided to 'wax the pole,' as you once put it, for that co-hosting promotion."

Seachest was taken aback by that comment. She appeared to him to truly enjoy the time they spent together lately and even though the promotion to co-host was the catalyst he used to get her out of her clothes, it never once crossed his mind the gig was the only thing keeping them off.

"I don't know what to say. So having sex with me is nothing more than a career opportunity to you?"

"Sorry, Bryan, but I'm all set in the love department. I have an amazing fiance who works with disadvantaged youth, but we were having trouble making ends meet on our combined low-level salaries. Now that

I'm going to be co-host of Taking Over with Bryan Seachest, we'll finally be able to move out of his parents' basement. So even though you coerced me, you're actually doing me a huge favor, and for that, I thank you."

That was it, then. He knew Erica wasn't his forever girl, but he didn't expect it to last for only as long as it took to process the paperwork and make her new job official. How dare she reject him! Again! The bitch had to go!

"No, Erica, it is I who should be thanking you for bringing to my attention our little 'arrangement' has an expiration date."

"What do you mean?" she asked, looking confused.

"You think you can sit there on my stool, wrapped in my blanket, in my dressing room, and tell me that your only interest in me is to fuck your way to the top? Honey, your ass is so delusional. And so fired!"

Erica was so surprised to hear those words she jumped up off the stool, knocking it over.

"What? You can't fire me! I've already signed a contract!"

Seachest reached into the couch cushions and pulled out a piece of paper.

"You mean this one?" he taunted her, as he tore it into pieces and threw it at her. "I'm afraid that never made it to payroll. What a shame. I guess the search for a new co-host is still ongoing."

"You bastard!" Erica shouted, lunging at him and starting to throw punches. Seachest was easily able to ward her off and tried not to laugh as he pushed her away.

"So much anger in such a small girl. If I were you, I'd consider my next move very carefully. As it stands, you've already seduced your boss in an effort to advance your career, and after finding out that didn't work, you've just physically assaulted me."

"You're the one who antagonized me!"

"Unless you can prove that, you're merely speaking in allegations. Now, as a former employee, I think it's best you leave."

Erica collected her clothes from the floor in a huff, looking like she was about to say something else but thought better of it. Keeping the blanket on her, she left the room while her former boss mockingly waved goodbye. When she was out of sight, Seachest's cellphone rang and since he was now alone, he got up off the couch naked and went to answer it.

"This is Seachest. Uh-huh. Uh-huh. You mean the porn star known as Red Velvet? That Briana Gifford? No kidding! Well, yeah. Absolutely! Of course I'll have her on the show! What's that? Dirt on the president? Even better! Tell her there's a guest spot for her whenever she can get here. You bet! Later!"

The universe never ceased to amaze him. One of his journalist contacts had just called with the interview of a lifetime! Briana Gifford, aka Red Velvet, was claiming to anyone who would listen that she slept with the president when she was only seventeen years old and had a mutual friend of theirs reach out to see if he, Bryan Seachest, king of all media, would be interested in having her discuss the situation on his radio show. Abso-fucking-lutely, he would! A political scandal discussed live, and he would be the one responsible for helping the victim's voice be heard while simultaneously creating more buzz around his show and his so-called "brand?" What an opportunity to just fall into his lap!

He checked himself out in the mirror, making sure his hair was properly mussed and there weren't any signs of dishevelment, before getting dressed and heading out into the world. Yup, life was definitely good.

<u>**Chapter 5**</u>

MOVIE-MAKING CAN BE a tough business. There are so many pieces that have to fall into place in the exact way everyone responsible for the project imagines for the final product to be just right. And not only are creatives and executive types banking on elements in the universe lining up in such a way as to make the movie possible, but between actors, behind-the-scenes crew, catering, scheduling, script supervision, and various other daily tasks that audiences rarely give thought to while they watch the narrative unfold on the screen before them, it's nothing short of a small miracle when production is wrapped and seen through to completion.

Ask any Hollywood veteran and they'd all agree a person would have to be nuts to want to make a career out of motion pictures. It's certainly not for Mr. Average Joe, who buckles easily under pressure, possesses little-to-no time-management skills, and can't lead a team to save his life. That's why entertainment mogul Carver Spleensteen considered himself a perfect fit for the industry. With a sharp eye for detail, a knack for cultivating talent, and the stamina to orchestrate everything from conception to distribution, Carver was a perfectionist when it came to his work, but he also knew when to be aggressive and when to lie low by letting somebody else take the reins. A passionate storyteller, he truly enjoyed discovering new voices and working with directors to bring exposure to their visions and guide them in the expansion of their careers. Plus, the money and notoriety were nice, too.

Acquiring power, though, can sometimes get to a person's head, leading to narcissism, an excessive sense of self-worth, and an air of entitlement which can come off as obnoxious and make said person difficult to be around. Enter Carver's brother, Todd. As much as Todd enjoyed movies and television shows growing up, he never necessarily aspired to partake in creating them. But the Spleensteen brothers were always close and when Todd began to notice the gradual change coming over Carver, the attitude, the irritable personality, and the "my way or the highway" approach to doing business, he knew he had to step in and help ease his brother's burden. Thus, a dual partnership, To The Max Films, was born.

Their studio was a literal overnight success, an unprecedented accomplishment for anyone in that line of work. Todd sought out scripts and worked with agents and managers, while Carver handled casting and dealing with talent. The first year of output from To The Max Films ranged from indie titles, *Slap You Silly, The Anglo-Saxon Conspiracy,* and *With This Dollar, I Thee Wed,* to more mainstream Oscar-nominated fare, *Back to New Hampshire, Girl on a String,* and *Pretty Little Princess.* By the time those movies were released and had broken box-office records worldwide, thereby making each project's cast bona fide stars, buzz quickly spread about the duo behind them, and To The Max Films was appropriately bringing in cash to the max for its owners. There was only one thing left to do, at least for Carver: indulge in some wannabe Hollywood Starlets.

Todd wasn't stupid or oblivious to his brother's manipulating ways, he just chose to pretend nothing was happening. As far as he was concerned, no acknowledgment meant no fallout, which meant nobody rocked the boat. Heading into the studio every day was business as usual, and productions stayed on track, bringing in more of that wonderful green paper both Spleensteens had gotten so used to. But Carver was becoming more reckless in his liaisons with the ladies, openly flaunting his connections and status in the industry and promising them one phone call from him was all it would take to make anyone's dreams come true. Some bought it and were putty in his hands, others indicated first needing some sort of proof, and some walked away in an attempt to call his bluff. Curiously, those particular ladies' names never went on to grace any small or large screens.

Carver was a pig all right, and other male celebrities and executive types would tell him to chill out and not be so eager to dominate his female actresses.

"You need to be smarter with how you go about your business," one once said.

"Pussy isn't worth putting your career in jeopardy over," warned another.

Yet, Carver's personal life was his concern alone. He always assured his friends and colleagues he knew what he was doing and was careful not to cross certain lines, but he'd never had access to such beautiful young women before, and there were some opportunities he simply couldn't let go to waste. The mirror in his bathroom reminded him what he looked like daily. He was nearly three hundred pounds, had a face only his mother ever loved, and was never one to find it easy to "spit game," as the kids called it. So what was a horny, straight, single man - who had never been married and whose longest relationship was with his hand - to do? Woo the aspiring actresses, of course! Some people found power an excellent aphrodisiac, and the way Carver's success helped him wield it was intoxicating! Maybe he was headed down a path of no return where the end of the road ended in regret and self-ruination, but damn if in the meantime he wasn't going to enjoy the ride!

Which brought him to today's casting call. The Spleensteens were holding open auditions for their next project, currently titled *Cam of*

Illusion, in a theater on their studio lot, and as per usual, were bickering with each other over who their next lead was of the girls they'd seen so far.

"We just found our lead, Todd!" Carver said to his brother. "The girl that was just in here killed it, and I won't hear you try to convince me otherwise!"

"You're crazy!" Todd replied. "Even though you deal with casting so much, sometimes you let your lust get the best of you and confuse aesthetic for talent! If it wasn't for me, our studio wouldn't be anywhere near as successful as it is."

"What? You think moviegoers are actually interested in talent nowadays? Bullshit! They want to see beautiful people up on that big screen. As long as they see beautiful people, the scene that plays out in front of them is irrelevant!"

"Yeah, maybe." Todd hated to admit it, but his brother made a good point. Soaps had been a major staple of daytime television for years, and having seen a few himself lately when he was at home with nothing else to do, he felt it safe to say people weren't tuning in for the acting.

"Not maybe. Definitely. That's why star power is a thing. Can you recall any decent scenes from the last few movies Johnny Depp's been in?"

Todd stayed silent and shrugged his shoulders, because no, he could not.

"Exactly," Carver continued. "But you still went to see them, right? And you know why? Because he's Johnny Fucking Depp and gay or straight, if that man asked you to put his dick in your mouth, you'd do it. That's my point. Beautiful people will overshadow talent every day of the week for as long as this industry continues to value brawn over brains. Now get your head out of your ass and I'll humor you by bringing in one more hopeful, but if she ends up being as bad as some of these others have been, we're going with my pick and calling it a day. Deal?"

"Fine. Deal."

"Hey, toots!" Carver called out to their assistant. "Who's next?"

"A Felicia Donner is next on the list, sir," the assistant said.

"Terrific! Send her in!"

The assistant disappeared and both Carver's and Todd's jaws dropped when their next audition entered the room.

"I take it you're Miss Donner?" Carver asked the young woman.

"That I am," Felicia replied.

"Well fuck me a million ways to Tuesday, darlin.' You're gorgeous!" Carver ran his tongue over his lips as he said that last part to emphasize he approved of her physique.

"Um, thanks," she said, looking a little weirded-out but determined to carry on.

"You're aware of what kind of movie this is, right?" Todd asked her.

"Yes, sir. I read the script and I'm here to audition as your leading lady."

"So having read the script, you're aware the lead role calls for nudity? Quite a bit of it, in fact," Todd said.

"Yes, sir. I noticed that."

"And that's something you're comfortable with?" Todd asked, wanting to make sure this girl knew exactly what she would be getting into.

"Totally! I really relate to the character here because I currently make most of my living as a cam girl, so depending on how much my viewers tip me, I'm naked most of the time anyway."

The two brothers gave each other a knowing look, as if silently agreeing they found their star. There was just one more matter that Carver, being Carver, wanted to address.

"How comfortable are you when it comes to...favors?" Carver asked Felicia.

"Favors, sir?" Felicia asked, confused.

"You know, sexual favors," Carver clarified.

"I'm afraid I don't understand. The script didn't read like it was porn."

"What my brother is trying to say is..." Todd tried to cut in before Carver cut him off.

"I've got this, Todd. Felicia, my dear, sometimes in Hollywood, when you're inches away from your big break, like you are right now, you need to seal the deal by performing an act of...appreciation, let's say."

A look of comprehension suddenly dawned on Felicia. She knew where this was headed and didn't intend for it to go any further, starting to walk away as Todd got up to stop her.

"Whoa! Hold on there!" Todd said. "Where are you going? I thought you wanted the part!"

"When you asked me if I was comfortable with nudity, I said yes. But I was referring to nudity on camera. I didn't think you meant right here, right now."

"Who said anything about getting naked right now?" Todd asked, feigning innocence.

"That man right next to you," Felicia said as she pointed to Carver, "implied I need to do something sexual for either one or both of you in order to get the part, and I haven't even read any of the character's lines yet. So obviously, this isn't the kind of audition I thought it was."

"You can leave on that high horse of yours if you want to, Miss Donner," Carver said, "but that really wouldn't be a good idea."

"Are you threatening me?" Felicia asked.

"Nothing of the sort. I'm only saying that nobody who's serious about a career in this industry walks out on Carver Spleensteen."

"Carver, would you just chill for a second? For fuck's sake!" Todd shouted.

"Eat shit, Todd! You're no innocent in this. You were ready to receive oral sex from her just as much as I was."

"Whoa! Hold on!" Felicia said, throwing her hands up in disgust. "Oral sex? For a movie role? You wish, you pervert!"

"You said you're a cam girl," Carver reminded her. "What's the difference?"

"The difference is the word, 'cam,'" the young woman replied. "There might be hundreds of people watching me strip at any given moment when I'm doing a web show, but I'm still just a girl on the internet at that point. I would never be expected to do anything with any of those viewers in real life!"

"That's too bad," said Carver, sounding disappointed. "I bet you'd be good at it."

"I'm out of here!" shouted Felicia, once more heading out of the room.

Carver sprang to his feet.

"If you leave now, I promise you your career will be over before it even begins!" he snarled.

"Whatever," Felicia said, flipping both brothers the bird and storming away.

Todd made to go after her but Carver pulled him back.

"Let her go, Todd."

"That didn't have to happen, you know. She was perfect for this role. We should have given it to her."

"That's exactly what I wanted to do."

"You know what I mean."

"I don't have patience for people that don't want to play by my rules," Carver said. "Besides, we have our lead, remember? We agreed if things didn't work out with this girl then we'd go with the previous one. And I'm sure she'd play ball."

"This is a really bad habit of yours," Todd said.

"Every once in a while can be likened to a bad habit, sure. But decades worth of young women under your belt because they know you're the gatekeeper of their hopes and dreams, that's no longer a habit. That's destiny. We've got a good thing going. We'd be fools not to take advantage."

Todd stood quiet before succumbing to his brother's justification.

"I can't argue with that," he said, sighing and accepting whatever Carver and fate had in store for him.

"Atta boy!" Carver threw his arms around his brother in a familial embrace and the two of them began to laugh. "Come on! We have some phone calls to make."

The Spleensteens headed back to their office, excited to get in touch with their new lead and begin hammering out the details of their next masterpiece.

<u>**Chapter 6**</u>

RENOWNED SCIENTIST AND TELEVISION personality Ted Toelash, "Triple T," Tiersen, was a pretty big deal in the scientific community, and it didn't make him sound arrogant or egotistical when he reminded people this was so. Most would scoff at the idea of someone bragging about their credentials or accomplishments so often to anyone and everyone who would listen, but it was somehow charming when Tiersen did it. Maybe people just respected his background and didn't care if he defined himself so much by his work, or maybe since he was black they didn't want to appear racist by criticizing him for the constant reminders everybody knew who he was. Tiersen authored several books on various subjects, ranging from space and time to history and evolution, made his rounds on both the daytime and late-night talk shows to promote his work and debate his scientific theories, and even hosted a local public access show for children, which in one of his drunken "fuck this, I'm tired of doing the same old shit" stupors, he decided to call, *Science, Blah,*

Blah, Blah. The ridiculous, lackadaisical title, which to him indicated ambivalence and a blasé approach to his hosting style, wound up receiving tons of praise, and the show itself even scored him an Emmy for excellence in children's programming. Talk about lax standards.

He never really aspired to be a Bill Nye-type as far as television and kids went, but if his books and talk show appearances made him a household name, it was, oddly enough, his children's show that really cemented celebrity status, as kids nationwide from ages five through twelve dubbed him the "father of science." Yes, that name actually came from his young viewers.

"Mommy, Daddy, I want to watch the father of science," his fans would say to their parents.

Four years in, *Science, Blah, Blah, Blah*, was a ratings juggernaut, spawning merchandise like Tiersen couldn't believe. He'd licensed his likeness and voice for things like clothes, comic books, and video games. Video games! Apparently today's children enjoyed playing educational, interactive games on their PlayStation and X-Box consoles. There were even murmurings about an animated series where he would voice the main character, a retired high school teacher tutoring troubled youth. It was all so surreal!

The truth was he hated hosting the TV show and couldn't understand why it was so popular. He went out of his way in each episode to explain as little as possible, choosing instead to focus on the more banal and mundane aspects of life like the sky being blue, the grass being green, and cars making loud noises when you over-revved their engines. Every day he went to the set and thought to himself, "Today will definitely be the day everyone sees how ridiculous this show is and cut me loose," but no such luck. The more pointless and seemingly disengaging an episode's topic was, the more critics praised it for its "authentic awareness of the world we live in." Damn! How the hell were there so many short-lived TV shows that got the chopping block every year? He couldn't get canceled no matter what he did! Again, a cynical part of him wondered if it was because he was black and nobody wanted to appear racist.

At least there was his production assistant, Cheyenne Sofarro, to look forward to being around. A black woman in her late twenties, Cheyenne had acted as Tiersen's right-hand woman behind the scenes for the past year, and getting to know her through the two of them working together served as the highlight of the show's production. Throughout the brief time they'd known each other, they'd attended several events together and speculation of the two of them being involved began running rampant. Tiersen was flattered the media and the general public even considered somebody like Cheyenne would go for a guy like him. He didn't consider himself bad-looking, but he was definitely much older than his PA and quite honestly, she wasn't his type. Sure, she was cute enough, maybe, in the right light, to some people who didn't know what attractive women were supposed to look like, but she had a small build and he preferred to go for the type that wouldn't make him feel as if he were making love to a child.

That's how he initially felt about her, anyway. But eventually, as tends to happen between two people working as closely together as he and Cheyenne did, the more he got to know her, the more he actually did begin to develop feelings for her. Small build or not, she was a woman and, therefore, possessed a vagina. He realized one day how long it had been since he'd last had sex and with that epiphany, an entirely different mindset started to take shape. All he needed was to get her alone. As often as they'd gone out to public events together, they were never by themselves and never received an opportunity to share an intimate moment. Which is why one day, in between takes of filming an episode, the following exchange took place.

"You know, Cheyenne, you should come by my place tonight and let me make you dinner," Tiersen suggested to his PA. "Give yourself a chance to relax and unwind."

"It's not that I don't want to, T," Cheyenne replied, "but not only are you old enough to be my father, you're also my boss. It wouldn't be appropriate."

"I just don't understand the logic behind that, Cheyenne. I take you out to business functions all the time. There have been more pictures taken of you and I together than there are of me and my ex-wife. I'm not asking you to marry me. I'm asking you to let me cook for you. Most women would be flattered by that."

"And I totally am. But think about this for a minute. You're not a stupid man. Us being seen together in public when it's work-related is one thing, but me being seen and potentially photographed by paparazzi going in and out of your home? People will talk, and it won't make either of us look good."

Tiersen started to get aggravated. Who was this woman to deny him, Triple T, father of prepubescent science, what he wanted? She was nothing! And without him, she would continue to be nothing! What an ungrateful little cunt!

"Fine! Whatever! If there's one thing Ted Toelash Tiersen doesn't do, it's beg! You don't want to accept my hospitality? Fuck you, then!"

Cheyenne was taken aback by her boss's harsh reaction and vulgarity. She had never heard him use that kind of language around her before.

"Whoa! Where is that coming from? Why are you taking this so personally?"

"You try taking someone under your wing and grooming them for nearly a year only to have them reject your romantic advances! My balls are blue, woman! And while that wasn't my initial intention, I'm zeroing in on you to provide me with a solution to that problem!"

"I can't believe you just said that to me!" Cheyenne scoffed. "Why in the hell would I care about your blue balls? Did you really think I was going to sleep with you? You're thirty years my senior, you pervert!"

Tiersen went on a rampage, shoving things off a nearby table, flipping things over, and generally trashing the set. Meanwhile, Cheyenne, visibly scared, backed away from him and cowered in fear, holding her hands in front of her face to protect herself from flying objects. The disturbance caused so much noise that one of the producers entered the room, demanding to know what was going on.

"What the hell is going on in here?" the producer shouted. "T, what's wrong? Why are you so upset?"

Tiersen stopped acting childish long enough to speak, but his words didn't answer his producer's question so much as create an accusation.

"I want this woman," he said, pointing to Cheyenne, "off my set and out of my sight!"

"What?" Cheyenne cried.

"You heard me!" Tiersen snarled. "I want you out of here!"

"We need her, T," the producer said. "She's part of the production crew. What happened? What did she do to upset you?"

"I'd rather not talk about it," Tiersen replied.

"Yeah, I bet you wouldn't!" Cheyenne snapped.

"Something obviously happened between you two, and someone better start providing me with some answers!" the producer yelled.

"She's a distraction on set and she makes me uncomfortable!" Tiersen said. "I don't want to work with her anymore!"

"I make you uncomfortable?" Cheyenne cried. "That's rich! What, are you afraid to tell one of your producers that you were hitting on me and went bat-shit crazy when I turned you down?"

"She's lying!" Tiersen insisted. "She was the one hitting on me and said she would say something to this effect if I didn't sleep with her!"

The producer stood there with his head in his hands for a second, exasperated and wondering how he now found himself as the mediator between two squabbling kids.

"Look," the producer finally spoke again after gathering his thoughts. "I don't care who wants to fuck who! We have a show to tape here, and we can't let any behind-the-scenes drama impede on our production schedule!"

The producer turned to Cheyenne.

"Nothing personal, kid, but that man's the star and you're not. Whatever the cause of the upset, I'm afraid I need to ask you leave."

"That's not far!" yelled Cheyenne. "I'm not guilty of doing anything other than my job!"

"As we all are," said the producer. "Listen, I'll make sure you get paid, okay? But if T's upset, he's not going to be able to smile big for the camera and teach science to children. Now, are you going to walk out with dignity, or do I need to call security?"

"I'm going! I'm going!" Cheyenne said, hands raised in defeat. As she made to leave, she turned back to her now-former boss. "This isn't over, T! Not by a long shot!" She stood there, staring him down for a moment, before making her exit.

The producer returned his attention to his star.

"Forget about telling me what happened. It's probably better I don't know anyway. If I get some people to clean this up, are you in the right mind to continue, or would you prefer to call it a day?"

"I'll be okay," Tiersen replied. "I just need to make a phone call. Something tells me I should have my lawyer on standby."

"I don't need to hear that, T," the producer said, putting his fingers in his ears. "In fact, I didn't hear that. Keep your thoughts to yourself and go do what you've got to do. Be back here in ten."

Tiersen left the set with the producer on his heels.

Just once, the producer thought as they went their separate ways, *it would be nice to work with someone who didn't let their celebrity status get to their head.*

Veronica Scarlett never saw herself in a serious relationship, being more committed to her work and jump-starting her career than to any one individual. She'd had some flings here and there, but nothing that ever lasted more than a handful of days or a couple of romps in the sack, whichever came first. Her family always knew she would grow up to be fiercely independent. If Veronica had been raised in a rural area with guns, she would very much have been the type to shoot first and ask questions later. She was loud, opinionated, unapologetic, and went after whatever she wanted. It didn't matter what challenges or obstacles she faced, being told she didn't stand a chance or that the odds were against her just made her more determined to prove everyone wrong.

She moved out to Los Angeles from her hometown of Atlanta, Georgia immediately after graduating high school and never looked back.

No Offense

The unknown was thrilling to her and she loved being a stranger to everyone she met, seeing her "nobody" status as a chance to start over. Two years later, still being a virtual nobody pissed her off, and she couldn't understand what she was doing wrong. She went to all the actor's workshops, all the open casting calls, and all the panels and festivals she could, attempting to network at every opportunity that presented itself to her. Nothing seemed to land. None of her auditions resulted in a callback, no one she brushed elbows with seemed to be interested in keeping in touch or pointing her in the right direction, and none of her fellow actors she auditioned with cared to even say as much as "hello." That is, until she met Jake.

At twenty-eight, Jake Asworth was several years older than her, but he was friendly, approachable, and handsome as well. All Veronica could think of when she first laid eyes on him was taking him for a ride, she could never have guessed that they'd be dating (the first relationship for her of its kind) by the end of that year. It was a casting call for a commercial advertising a new pet product for cat owners called Over Rice. Similar to a litter box, a container of some sort would get filled with real uncooked rice, and mixed in with the grains of rice would be fragments of soap that would expand when added to water to serve as a portable bathtub for the cat. Even though cats are naturally adverse to water, the joke was an owner would have his or her cat literally over rice, thus making the concept a novelty product more than anything else. Jake and Veronica happened to both be auditioning as the cat owner in the commercial and got to talking while they awaited their turns.

Jake was a Los Angeles native, born and raised in the area and garnering the desire to be in the spotlight throughout his life. Unlike Veronica, he didn't let his aspirations blow up his ego or lead to an overly huge sense of self, which made him one of the most down-to-earth and relatable people she had ever met. He told her he lived in a nearby studio apartment and waited tables to pay the bills while juggling auditions around his work schedule. Veronica, who up to that point had only been bringing in money by doing odd jobs here and there and never knew where she was going to end up at the end of any given day, had jokingly mentioned her situation and asked if the restaurant Jake worked at was hiring. Not only did she find herself in Jake's bed that night, but it turned out his employer was indeed looking for an extra set of hands, and the two had been dating, living, and working together ever since. As for the commercial, it never went into production and the Over Rice product itself was pulled from all store shelves, never to be sold again, after the animal rights group PETA got involved and claimed the product, novelty or not, mixing cats and rice together sent a bad message to the general public. Apparently, the group's members were unaware of Chinese food.

So it was that Jake found himself with a new live-in girlfriend and Veronica found herself with not only her first serious boyfriend, but her first permanent home since moving out west. She was grateful to Jake for taking her in and the events that had played out since, but another two years had passed since their fateful encounter, and neither seemed to be any closer to hitting the big time. They were trying to forget their sorrows over a board game one day when Veronica, being Veronica, came up with an interesting scenario in her mind she just had to let Jake in on.

"Okay, Jake, here's an interesting thought for you. You're watching a split-screen monitor with two different rooms. In one room is a baby sleeping in its crib and in the other is an elderly couple sitting on a couch and holding hands. Unknown to either of their occupants, both rooms are entirely electrified. You're given a small controller with two different buttons and told one will fry the baby, and the other will fry the couple. You have sixty seconds to decide which button to press or both rooms light up and all three of them die. Which one do you choose, and why?"

Jake put down the dice he was about to roll as he prepared to take his turn and stared at his girlfriend, confused.

"Damn, Veronica! That's so dark and kind of came out of nowhere! You should pitch that idea for the next *Saw* movie."

"I'll take that as a compliment," Veronica said, laughing. "Now, answer the question. Which room goes up in fireworks?"

"Why are we talking about this?" Jake asked, still confused.

"I want to take a break from the game we're playing and do another one. It's a verbal game called What Would You Do?"

"Okay, still a bit out of nowhere, but I'll play along."

"So choose."

"Well, neither option is a good one."

"That's the point!" Veronica said, trying to explain herself. "But both rooms are screwed anyway if you don't pick one or the other, so which is it?"

"Hmm...if I absolutely had to choose, and you're telling me I do for the sake of the game, right?"

"Right."

"Then I guess I'd have to kill off the elders. They've already lived their lives, but the baby's just a baby."

"Now let me throw you a curveball," Veronica said. "The elderly couple is in perfect health, and each of them easily has a couple of decades left in them, if not more. The baby was born with a rare genetic disorder that's going to make life increasingly difficult for it as it gets older, and it will likely lead a very frustrating and miserable life. It will never be able to live alone, always be dependent on others, and just generally hate its existence. With that in mind, do you still kill off the couple, knowing that their lives are going to be much happier and more productive than whatever kind of a life the baby will lead?"

"Jesus Christ!" Jake said, looking at Veronica like she was some sort of maniacal serial killer. "I don't want to play this game anymore!"

"Come on! Just humor me for this one instance and then we go can go back to Monopoly. I promise."

Jake sat silent for a second, contemplating his response.

"Well, that's a hell of a spot to be in, killing off a child with a disease or killing off a perfectly healthy couple. But I still think the child deserves a chance at life."

"Oh, I see. You're one of those," Veronica mocked her boyfriend.

"One of what?" he asked, defensively.

Veronica answered in a tauntingly high-pitched voice.

"We can't kill the baby because it's an innocent, regardless of the useless life it might lead," she said, laughing afterwards. "One of those."

"Fine! I'll let the couple live!" Jake snapped, momentarily angry.

"Are you happy?"

"I can't believe I just talked you into killing a baby!" Veronica continued laughing. "You're so easily manipulated!"

"Well, the more I think about it, the more I agree with you. If the couple's perfectly healthy and still has plenty of time left, it doesn't make sense to sacrifice them for a kid that's never going to be able to realize its true potential."

"If we ever end up having a kid of our own, remind me to never tell you about its medical history."

"Ha ha. Very funny."

Veronica's cellphone began to ring. On the other end was her best friend she'd known since middle school, Courtney Coccyx.

"Hey, Court! What's up?" Veronica asked, answering her phone, as Jake was briefly subjected to only one side of the conversation. "What's that? I'm having trouble hearing you. Hold on. I'm going to put you on speaker."

She put the phone on speaker and placed it on the table between her and Jake.

"Okay, you're on speaker now," she said to her friend. "And be forewarned, Jake's here too, so you can't go on any rants about what a loser he is."

"Veronica! You know I would never do that!" Courtney exclaimed.

"I would hope not!" Jake said.

"Hi, Jake!"

"What's up, Courtney?"

"Did I interrupt anything?"

"Nothing sexual, if that's what you mean," Veronica said. "I was just presenting Jake with a little verbal scenario called What Would You Do?"

"Your friend here is pretty sick in the head, Courtney," Jake said. "I worry about her sometimes."

"Don't we all," Courtney replied.

"Anyway," Veronica cut in, not wanting to be the focus of the conversation. "What was it you were trying to say a minute ago?"

"Oh, yeah. I was asking if you'd heard about this 'Good to Go' law. The president apparently wants to sleep with a minor he met and is urging Congress to do away with the age of consent. At least, according to TMZ."

"No shit!" Jake blurted out.

"Seriously?" Veronica asked.

"It's all over the news. They're fast-tracking the bill and plan to vote on it tomorrow. Everybody's talking about it. I'm surprised you didn't know."

"We don't watch much TV," Veronica said.

"Well, don't you read the news online?" Courtney asked.

"When we're on the computer, but we've been staring at the computer screen almost 24/7 the last couple of days sending out head shots and resumes for auditions, so we took a break from it today."

"Figures when we decide to do that something of importance actually happens," Jake said.

"Well, my family hates it when I talk politics and I had to vent to somebody, so I called you."

"I'm flattered," Veronica said, her tone oozing with sarcasm.

"You should be," her friend insisted.

"Okay, so go ahead," Veronica said to her bestie. "Start venting."

"Well, I'm like, totally disgusted by this, aren't you? It's hard enough to be a woman and deal with everything we deal with, and now adolescents and pre-teens might not be safe anymore from sexual predators? It's not right!"

"So let me guess, you don't support the bill?" Veronica asked.

"How could I? Just thinking about it makes me want to like, totally throw up in my mouth!"

"Don't hate me too much for saying this," Veronica said, "but would it really be the end of the world if kids learned the facts of life a little ahead of schedule?"

"Veronica!" Courtney exclaimed, surprised at her best friend. "You must be joking!"

"Relax! Of course I am," Veronica assured her. Then paused

before ending with, "kind of."

"Well, I'm not too big on politics myself, Courtney," Jake chimed in, "but I agree with you. That's pretty fucked up!"

"Right? It's like this president's only hobbies aside from golf are watching TV and conspiring to make people's lives hell!"

Veronica was losing interest in the conversation and wanted an excuse to end it, so she put her hand on Jake's thigh and started rubbing it.

"And on that note, Court," she said, making circular motions on her boyfriend's leg in a way that suggested it was time for Ride 'Em Cowboy, "I think Jake and I might end up doing something sexual after all, so I'm gonna let you go."

"Wait, before I forget!" Courtney said. "Have you ever heard of the porn star that went by the name Red Velvet?"

"Fuck yeah! That woman's movies are amazing!" Jake said, before Veronica gave him a look indicating she didn't approve. "So I've been told," he corrected himself.

"Well, at least one of us is familiar with her," Veronica said, turning her attention back to her phone. "Why? What does she have to do with this?"

"She just gave an interview on Taking Over with Bryan Seachest, where she claimed the president took advantage of her during a beauty pageant he ran when she was just seventeen years old, and paid her off so she would never tell anyone!"

"Sounds to me like she owes him his money back then," Veronica said, seemingly indifferent to Courtney's reveal.

"Come on, Veronica, have a heart," Jake said. "The woman's claiming she was pressured into having sex with a powerful man. She was probably really intimidated."

"Look, I'm not saying I'm glad it happened to her, but the woman's gotta be what, late forties, maybe even early fifties now? Does it really matter that she's coming forward all these years later? So our president's a pig! It's not like he hasn't already proven that in the past. Personally, I'm not surprised he would bed a minor."

"It's not the allegation that's newsworthy, Veronica," Courtney said. "It's what the allegation translates to in terms of the man's character and overall motivation. If he was willing to break the rules before he was given the keys to the White House, you better believe he's willing to break them now, when he's in a position where it's even easier for him to do so."

"Wow, that was deep," Veronica replied.

"Do you ever take things seriously?" Jake asked his girlfriend. "In the two years we've been together, I don't think I've ever seen you take anything seriously."

"And yet you took me back here the day we met and rode me like a roller coaster. You must really love me."

Courtney decided she'd had enough of the conversation too and made to wrap it up.

"I'm gonna go now. Just thought you might be interested in what's going on in the outside world. I know how you actors are. Bye, Girlie!"

"Later, Court!" Veronica ended the call and placed the phone into her pants pocket.

"Pretty crazy stuff, huh?" Jake asked. "You think Red Velvet's claim is true?"

"I'd be more surprised if it wasn't true," Veronica replied. "Like I said before, the president's past isn't exactly a secret."

"But can you imagine if it really was a lie?" Jake continued, trying to process everything he just heard. "Going public with a fake story like that to put yourself in the spotlight and tarnish someone else's reputation? That would be brutal!"

Veronica remained quiet.

"Do you think you'd ever be capable of something like that?" Jake asked.

"You mean would I be able to make light of rape for personal gain?"

"That's exactly what I mean. Would you?"

Veronica was silent for a moment before responding.

"Hmm...Honestly, I don't know," she said, then quickly clarified when she saw the look on Jake's face. "Come on! I'm kidding! Of course I would never do that!"

Appearing satisfied with her answer, Jake got up to use the bathroom and prepare for the session of love Veronica mentioned the two of them were going to partake in prior to them concluding their conversation with Courtney. When he was out of earshot, Veronica said quietly to herself, "Not unless I felt I had a very good reason."

<u>**Chapter 7**</u>

THERE'S NO BEDROOM LIKE a presidential bedroom, because it's the only bedroom anywhere that can lay claim to hosting the President of the United States when he's at his most vulnerable. It was late at night and the president was dressed in his pajamas, guard down, and reminiscing about the events of the past day. He was scrolling through his social media feed on his phone when he received a call from his boyhood friend, Vlad Putrid, and eagerly answered it.

"Vladdy Boy! I was just thinking about you the other day! How have you been?"

"Busy," his Russian friend replied, blunt and to the point. "In Russia we actually have things that need tending to in order to keep our homeland functioning properly. Plus, we are still acting as a refuge for one of your own, a fact my friends give me crap for on a daily basis."

The individual Vlad was referring to was considered a traitor to the U.S. for gathering operational monitoring tactics during his time at the

NSA. He eventually fled the country with the information, but not before leaking it to the press so that the entire populace knew what their government was up to – spying on all electronic correspondence such as emails and texts to see if anyone was secretly in contact with known terrorists. The man responsible for going public with this information wasn't necessarily a bad or dangerous guy, and government agents perusing said correspondence weren't necessarily corrupt or shady people, but nonetheless, Americans had now been made aware that messages they thought were private weren't so, and the shit hit the fan after that.

Aware of the reputation he'd made for himself after making such tactics public, the individual in question knew he couldn't stay in the country and sought out refugee status in Russia, of all places, as if POTUS's relationship with Vlad wasn't bad enough lately. Vlad, of course, took him in, eager to know what had caused him to garner such a reputation back home, and considered him a valuable source of information, so he allowed him to stay. That was a subject POTUS didn't want to expand on with Vlad, so he let the comment fly.

"And yet as busy as you claim to be, you still find time for your favorite American," the president joked. "I'm touched, Vladdy, really."

"Why I call is no joking matter, my friend," Vlad said, wanting to keep the reason for his call on topic. "What is this I am hearing about a Good to Go Law?"

"Nothing you need to concern yourself with," the president said. "My decisions are outside of your jurisdiction."

"Oh, yes?" Vlad asked, starting to sound upset. "This is not the impression you gave me when you came seeking my help a few years ago."

"There was already an investigation that concluded you had nothing to do with the final count," the president told his buddy. *And that's all they'll ever prove*, he thought to himself. "Besides, we promised to have each other's backs, remember?"

"And when have you had my back, hmm?" Vlad asked angrily. "With you, it is always take, take, take. Three years as President of United States and you have yet to do anything to benefit Russia! I'm beginning to think our arrangement was a mistake!”

The president couldn't believe what he was hearing.

“Nothing to benefit Russia? I love you too much to get into an argument with you, Vladdy, but just my mere presence here prevents you from having to deal with a woman in matters of diplomacy! You're welcome!”

“You know what I mean! When we met years ago, I expressed my dislike of your country and you promised me Russia would rise as a greater power on the world stage. I grow impatient waiting for this to happen!”

“Are you living under a rock over there? Have you not paid attention to anything I've done throughout my presidency? I've added two trillion dollars to the national debt, I ignore pretty much all issues that come across my desk in favor of watching TV and golfing, and I'm doing my best to antagonize countries into going to war. It's all for you, Vladdy! I swear!”

Vlad was silent for a moment. Perhaps his American friend, in his own way, was doing his best to turn his country inside-out after all.

“This...pleases me,” Vlad said after quiet thought. “I have, of course, heard of your antics, but like the rest of the world, I considered them mere child's play. I suppose it did not cross my mind that your particular brand of mock leadership might actually be working in my favor after all. Forgive me, comrade.”

“Never doubt me. That's all I'm saying.”

“I yield. My anger was premature. We can forget this happened, yes?”

“Of course, Vladdy! We're buddies! I could never stay mad at you!”

“Glad to hear it! Now, you must still tell me about this 'Good to Go' proposal. I want to make sure I understand it correctly because I'm thinking of adopting a similar law here. You are essentially looking to score young pussy without any legal repercussions, yes?”

“You got it!”

“A brilliant idea, honestly! Kids these days are so promiscuous, it is hard to find a virgin to break in. But if you can go younger, I imagine the odds become much greater."

"I don't even care about the virgin thing," the president said. "That doesn't make a difference to me."

"Then I'm confused," Vlad said. "What is the point of this law if not to take away children's innocence?"

"Well, Vladdy, I don't know if you happened to see the picture that went viral, but I met a girl. A beautiful, sexy, perfectly proportioned girl, and as the law currently stands, I can't make a move on her or anyone else like her until she's eighteen. That's the age you're officially considered an adult here."

"Ah, I see. So I take it this girl isn't eighteen."

"She's sixteen. When I found out, I proposed the bill immediately. I don't wait for anything I want, much less two years."

"Very interesting. And what do your constituents think of this law?"

"My who?" the president asked, not having a clue as to whom Vlad was referring.

"Focus, comrade! The voters! Your fellow citizens! The ones you rule over! What do they think of this bill? Do they support your pursuit of young tail?"

"The ones that agree with me will embrace anything I do. The ones that don't, fuck 'em! And besides, this isn't an issue open for public debate. Congress votes on the bill tomorrow. They're the only ones who need to agree with me that this is the right thing to do. And I have no doubt they will."

"And what of your wife? What does she think about this?"

"Nadia keeps to herself at all times, and if she ever has an opinion, she doesn't express it to me. She knows better."

Unbeknownst to the president throughout his conversation with Vlad, his wife, Nadia, was standing in the doorway towards the back of the room. She had only heard the tail end of what was discussed, but it was enough to know she didn't like the topic or the way her husband chose to do business. Sure, she knew what she signed up for when she agreed to marry the man, and that was all good and fine when she could lead her own private life while he played Mr. Hollywood and real estate mogul, but she never agreed to live a life of constant scrutiny in the White House as the First Lady while her husband decided to "try this politics thing," as he had said when he initially told her he decided to run for office.

Their lives hadn't been the same the last few years. Publicly they were united, privately they were divided, and she believed she had the American political system to thank for that. Her husband was far from perfect and came with baggage like everybody else, but he meant well, she had to keep telling herself. Because if he didn't mean well, if his intention was to screw over the people that made him who he was and truly defer to overseas autocrats and dictators, then the country, as well as the world, were about to write chapters of history that not even she could hope to have any influence over. Somehow, day by day, she managed to hold onto her faith, but it was getting harder as time went on.

And then there was the situation with her step-daughter. Nadia wasn't as oblivious to things as people thought; she knew what went on between her husband and Yolanda. She cringed at the thought of it, of course, but figured there wasn't much she could do. Was she supposed to just barge into his bedroom, catch them in the act, and hope that they'd both be so embarrassed they'd stop doing those kinds of things with each other? Fat chance! Nothing like the bond between father and daughter after all, right? No matter how overly close they let that bond become. Nadia intended to stay on the sidelines and let things unfold however they saw fit. She didn't plan to have any incestuous affairs with her offspring. Hell no! But if that was how powerful men chose to do things in America, then whatever. As long as she stayed pampered and clothed in her favorite designer brands, nothing else mattered.

She turned to leave and passed Yolanda in the hall, no doubt on her way to her father's room for another session of their nightly activities. Yolanda tried covering her face with her hand as they passed each other, as if there was no way Nadia would recognize her step-daughter in that robe of hers just by the mere act of her left hand covering her left cheek. But again, whatever. Who cares, right? The leader of the free world and his flesh and blood had a special relationship nobody would understand, but that didn't make it wrong.

Happy go lucky, Nadia thought. *I'm as free as a bird. Nothing's bothering me. Blah, blah, blah.* She almost had herself convinced of this fictional truth as she took a deep breath, started to envision the bed that awaited her in the East Wing without a man nearly twice her age in it, and continued on her way to her private quarters.

The nation's capitol is simultaneously a beautiful and ugly place, perhaps the only area in the entire country that can stake claims to such polar opposites at once. Our Founding Fathers did great things on the Hill, and the United States of America owes much to them for their historic feats and visionary rulings. But if any of them were alive today, they would be greatly saddened and disappointed to find the laws they laid down centuries ago are now interpreted not for what they actually say, but for how those written words will benefit whichever party is trying to gain something from them. Enter our modern-day politicians.

Capitol Hill found itself full of old men with a point to prove and an agenda to fulfill when the time came to debate the merits of the president's proposed Good to Go Law. Candy Baloney, an elderly lady in her early eighties who had risen to Speaker of the House through her many years of public service, and realized she was the only female in the room that day, didn't care for the bill one bit. Unlike her male colleagues, she recognized a terrible idea when she heard one, and the Good to Go Law, if passed, would be absolutely awful. She couldn't support this bill in good conscience, but it didn't surprise her that so many people did. Even some fellow women she knew with grandchildren and young daughters didn't see a problem with allowing "love to be love," as they put it. People were dumb. It was as simple as that. Regardless of her personal biases, however, she had a job to do, so she called what she considered the sham meeting to order.

"Everybody, settle down!" Baloney shouted, pounding a mallet.

"Take your seats so we can get started, please."

Everyone present took a seat and settled in for the task at hand.

"Now, we all know why we're here," Baloney continued. "I take no pleasure in reminding you of this, but there's a bill that's been proposed currently being referred to as the Good to Go Law, and it's up to us to decide its future. I have a feeling I already know exactly how this is going play out, but I'd be a hypocrite if I didn't at least go through the motions and pretend to care, so let's just get right to it."

One of the older men, whose name tag read "Useless Congressman Four" raised his hand. (It was decided a while ago that placards in front of them baring their names when they gathered was childish, so some genius came up with the idea of wearing name tags instead and for some reason, that struck everyone as simply brilliant.)

"This isn't a classroom, Congressman," Baloney sighed. "If you have something to say, just say it."

"I want to be officially recognized," Useless Congressman Four replied. "Isn't that how this is supposed to work?"

"Fine," Baloney said, rolling her eyes. "Useless Congressman Four has the floor."

"Thank you, your honor."

"This isn't a courtroom either, Congressman."

"I'm just trying to be polite."

"Whatever," Baloney said, head in her hands. "Make your point. Out with it."

"I just wanted to say I think this bill has a lot of potential so I support it, and I think everyone here today should too."

Useless Congressman Four's statement was met with wild applause and whistling.

"So an old man supports being able to stick it to a little girl," Baloney taunted him. "Shocking. I'm starting to wonder if there's even a point to these proceedings. Is there anyone here aside from myself who doesn't want the bill to pass?"

They all looked around the room at each other, nobody making an effort to raise their hand or speak up in opposition of the bill. Suddenly, a man whose name tag read "Useless Congressman Six" began to speak.

"What is wrong with you people?" he asked. "How could you even give this bill serious consideration? Don't you all have wives and families? Wouldn't any of you be the least bit ashamed to talk to your grandchildren and tell them it's now legal to have boyfriends and girlfriends their parents' age?"

"Finally!" Baloney exclaimed. "A voice of reason! You, Congressman Six, are not useless!"

"I wouldn't go that far," Useless Congressman Six said. "As government employees, we're all pretty useless to some degree or another, but this is about ethics and morals. My friends, I ask you to put aside your libidos for one minute. If a twelve-year-old girl came home one day and announced she was pregnant because she'd been having an affair with one of her teachers, does anyone here really think that would be okay?"

"If she wasn't raped and it was consensual, why not?" asked Useless Congressman One.

"Because adults shouldn't be having babies with babies! Can't you sick fucks realize that?" shouted Useless Congressman Six.

"Who says I'm sick if love decides to take me down a slightly unconventional route?" Useless Congressman One continued. "Teenage girls were married, barefoot, and pregnant all of the time in the Middle Ages. And don't forget, this law would apply to girls and boys, so if a young man wanted to hit on an older woman, he would now be able to. And if the older woman was interested, she wouldn't have to risk jail time by saying yes. This bill, if it becomes law, is meant to bring people together, Congressman. That's why I'm all for it."

The gathered congressmen started arguing among themselves, with the majority who supported the bill trying to convince those who didn't why they should allow it to pass.

"ENOUGH!" Baloney shouted, attempting to regain control of the room. Everyone became quiet and directed their attention to the Speaker. "Let's make this quick and easy since we get paid the same either way, shall we? No arguing, no more shouting, just a show of hands."

"I thought you said this wasn't a classroom," said Useless

Congressman Four.

"It is now," said Baloney. "Since you're all clearly incapable of explaining yourselves without regressing to the behavior of your youth, listen to me very carefully. There's only one question here that's important. How many of you want this proposed law to pass? Raise your hand."

Ten of the twelve congressmen present raised their hands. The two who didn't were Useless Congressman Six, who already made his case, and a new voice to the mix, Useless Congressman Nine.

"Well, we already know where this vote is headed, don't we?" Baloney said, after scanning the room. "But humor me, Number Nine. Why are you siding with Congressman Six?"

"Because it's the right thing to do," Useless Congressman Nine replied.

"My ass!" Useless Congressman One snapped. "You just don't want to admit to yourself that you're as perverted as the rest of us! Come on over to the dark side. We've got candy, and soon we'll have pre-teen pussy!"

"Congressman One," Baloney said. "I have to ask, to satiate my own curiosity, you understand, do you already have an underage girlfriend?"

"What?" Useless Congressman One said, sounding offended. "No way!"

"I was just wondering. Because you see, there are a couple of claims you've made already that put me under the impression you can't wait for this law to pass so you can then trot out your young lady like a prized pony at the county fair!"

"Damn it, Baloney!" Useless Congressman One yelled. "None of us are on trial here! Think what you want, but judging by the vote we just took, looks to me like we've got us a new law!"

"You can be better than the president, Number One," Useless Congressman Nine said. "You can rise above your desires."

"I really can't," Useless Congressman One responded.

"Everyone, please!" Baloney pleaded, naively hoping she could still turn the situation around. "I implore you to rethink what we're about to do here. If this law goes into effect, it will essentially nullify all the other laws that have been put in place against child molesters and sexual predators. Do we really want to give those types of people license to prey on the younger generation?"

"I'm okay with that," Useless Congressman Two said.

"Yeah, so am I," agreed Useless Congressman Five.

"Works for me," Useless Congressman Seven chimed in.

"Ditto," echoed Useless Congressman Eight.

"Fine," Baloney sighed. "I can't believe I'm about to say this, but the motion passes. The 'Good to Go' bill is hereby considered approved. This session of Congress is adjourned."

The Speaker banged her gavel to signify an end to the meeting and the room began to empty as everyone got up to leave. Baloney chose to remain in her seat and waited until she was alone to shake her head in dismay.

I am so not looking forward to talking to reporters about this, she thought to herself. *The press coverage is going to be a disaster.*

The president woke up the next morning feeling pretty damn good. He had done it! The single most important piece of legislation in the history of his administration so far, the Good to Go Law, had been passed by Congress, and now it was time to gloat.

He headed out of his residence toward the White House Rose Garden, where he expected to find a scene similar to the one in the press room the other day - rows and rows of reporters and admirers chomping at the bit to ask him questions and congratulate him on getting a bill passed so quickly. But as he approached the podium that was set up, he was disappointed to find the only things greeting him were a single camera and his press secretary, Tara Blanders.

"What the hell is this?" the president asked, frustrated.

"It seems nobody from the media cares to hear you brag about what most consider to be a filthy law, sir," Tara said to her boss.

No Offense

"Are you fucking kidding me? One of the best days of my political career and they're really not gonna let me enjoy it? Heartless bastards! Who am I talking to with this camera, then?"

"I've taken the liberty of setting up a camera of my own to record whatever you want to say, and then I figured I would send copies of the tape to the local news affiliates. All we need is one network interested in running it for the others to decide to run it too. Nobody wants to be scooped."

"Fine," the president said, rolling his eyes. "As long as I can still get a message to the American people. My supporters deserve to hear this victory is theirs as much as mine."

Tara headed behind the camera, pressed record, and gave the signal for the president to begin his prepared statement.

"I'm pleased to announce Congress has decided to do the right thing and pass the Good to Go Law. This is going to be the start of something huge, believe me. I can already tell you so many people are excited for this thing to finally take effect. People have wanted a law like this for pretty much ever, and I'm happy to be the one to make it a reality for them.

"Love has always been blind, but now it's also ageless. And who's the one that made it so? That's right! Me! So the next time you're wondering if that hot little number you just encountered could be your future, even if she's only in grade school, go for it! Entice her. Lure her in any way you can think of. Show her the benefits of being with an older man. And when you finally have her right where you want her, and you're doing things that before you could only dream about, you can think of me, your humble president.

"God bless you all! And God bless the United States of America! Thank you!"

Tara stopped recording once the president finished speaking and just stood there, staring at him, with a clear mix of bewilderment and disgust on her face.

"I'll be honest with you, sir. I'm not sure if anyone's going to want to air that statement. At least, not without some very delicate editing."

77

"Then we'll post it online, uncut. We can put it on the White House YouTube channel and I'll post it on my personal social media profiles. It's more likely to find its audience on the internet anyway."

"Sir, I'm not really sure if..."

"Make it happen!" the president cut her off. "And if you won't, I'll find someone else who will. Remember what I told you when I first offered you this gig? I tell you what to do and you do it. Simple. So, go! Now!"

The president headed back toward the White House, eager to return to his residence and see what kind of waves the Good to Go Law was making on the television news circuit. Tara collected the camera containing the video message that was just shot and decided to take it to the one network she knew almost always had a slot available for her boss, BNN, the Biased News Network.

Chapter 8

THE NAME STEWIE YZ used to mean something. Like all good artists of their craft, it wasn't just a name, it was a brand. At the height of his career, YZ had a successful primetime television sitcom, performed and toured to sold-out venues all around the globe, and even enjoyed a stint as a best-selling author with the release of his memoir, *Hold This For Me*, back in 2014. Now, not even a full decade later, things had changed, and not for the better. Too many people considered themselves "woke" (whatever the fuck that meant), and YZ's particular brand of humor that used to score big laughs and make him universally beloved started to stall. The concept of "cancel culture," where those who disagreed with an artist's views decided to make it their personal mission to ensure said artist no longer had a career, thereby "canceling" them, swept throughout the entertainment industry, making it extremely difficult for comedians like YZ to continue to do what he did best.

But tonight, as YZ took to the stage for the first time in three years to test out new material he was hoping would lead to a new comedy special and tour, he figured he had some guaranteed hits on his hands. The country's current commander-in-chief may have proven himself completely inept at handling the nation's affairs, but for late-night talk show hosts, sketch comedy shows, and various other comedians, he was comedic gold that practically begged for those who did jokes for a living to incorporate his foul-ups into their routines. YZ was all too happy to answer that call and take some of that gold for himself. Hence, here he was, about to unleash a barrage of invectives about the president he was certain would put him right back on the map.

"What a great world we live in, huh?" YZ began his set. "You don't need to be qualified for anything anymore. You can literally just take whatever you want and do whatever you want. You want to declare yourself CEO of a family-run business even though you've never been responsible for anything a day in your life? Go for it! It's all you! Nepotism's a beautiful thing! Hell, you can even be President of the United States with absolutely zero background in politics!"

The audience responded positively to what they heard. They were cheering, laughing, and generally enjoying themselves. *So far so good*, YZ thought.

"And not only do you need no experience to be considered the head of the most powerful country on the planet, but it comes with some pretty fucking sweet perks. Porn star pussy, for one. Have you guys heard about this?"

The room was suddenly silent, indicating YZ was losing the audience's support, but he didn't get where he was by not taking risks, so he plowed ahead as planned.

"Not only has Red Velvet come out publicly about her affair with the president, but she says it happened when she was just a teenager. I mean, no wonder he came up with the 'Good to Go' law. I'm sure that's an experience he's looking forward to repeating."

Still silence. YZ was starting to feel as uncomfortable as those in attendance.

"Wow. Tough crowd. I didn't know there were so many

presidential supporters here tonight. But that's okay. That's the purpose of trying out new material. You find out what works and what doesn't."

"You suck, YZ!" shouted a middle-aged female audience member who encouraged the crowd to begin booing.

"Nobody told you to come out tonight, lady!" YZ shouted back, switching to survival mode. "You knew who was on the roster and you came anyway, so you must not think I'm that bad!"

"This is an open mic event!" the woman shouted again. "There was no roster!"

"Touche," YZ said, calming down in an attempt to save face and his performance. "What's your name, darling?"

"You mean you don't remember me?" the woman asked.

"I've got a bunch of light shining on me up here which virtually guarantees I can't see past the front row, but I'll admit to recognizing your voice."

"Does the name Casey Forthright ring a bell?" she asked, standing up and folding her arms across her chest.

YZ's eyes went wide and a look of panic crossed his face. That name did indeed hold meaning for him. Casey was a fan of his, or used to be anyway, who got to meet him after one of his shows during his last tour when she won a backstage pass through a radio contest. She was a bit older and had a body type different than what he usually went for, but being that life for a traveling comedian presented very few opportunities to get laid, he took her to his dressing room and attempted to get himself some relief. Unfortunately for him, much as she claimed to like him and his work, Casey wasn't that type of woman, and after some coaxing, the most he got her to do was lift up her shirt and flash him while he masturbated to the sight of her tits, which were a decent size and impressively perky for her age.

When he was finished and they were both fully clothed again, he offered to take a picture with her and sign anything she would like. Disgusted by what had just happened, she declined and made her exit. He wasn't proud of what he did and considered chasing after her to apologize, but he couldn't think of a way to make the situation any better, so he let her go and decided to forget about it, figuring he would never see her again anyway. Now, here she was, and her presence was less than welcome during a night that was supposed to help revitalize his career. There was only one thing he could think to do: bail.

"I'm afraid that's all I have for tonight," he said, placing the microphone back in its stand. "Thanks for coming out, everyone!"

"What's wrong, YZ?" Forthright taunted him. "Afraid to confront your past? Joking around at the president's expense and hoping your own issues won't come to light?"

YZ ignored his heckler and headed backstage.

"That's right! Walk away, you pervert!" Forthright continued. "Who's waiting for you back there? Someone else that's agreed to watch you masturbate for kicks?"

The booing stops as the audience listens intently. They weren't expecting anything like this.

"Stewie YZ is a misogynist, ladies and gentleman," Forthright told the audience. "He says he appreciates all of his fans, but if he can't show you his genitalia, he wants nothing to do with you!"

YZ decided enough was enough and rushed back out to the mic.

"Look, I'm not perfect, okay? But I'm obviously not the only one. What about our president, hmm? Why can he get away with things the rest of us can't? If you want to call me a pig, fine! I'm a pig! But what about our lovely commander-in-chief? If the president can do it then damn it, I should be able to do it, too!"

YZ threw the mic on the ground this time and flipped the crowd the bird as he headed backstage again amid more booing. So much for the all-American comeback.

Footage from what became dubbed "the infamous YZ performance" started making its rounds online, going viral within hours of being uploaded and making Stewie YZ a household name once more, just not in the way he envisioned. The clip played on various talk shows and news programs, painting YZ as a poison to the entertainment industry and forcing him to cancel all upcoming projects and appearances.

"The best thing you can do for yourself right now," a friend told him, "is just lie low and stay out of sight."

So that's exactly what he chose to do. But try as he might to put that night behind him, the footage kept popping up everywhere, even on the primetime news.

"This was the scene during one of Stewie YZ's performances at a local comedy club just the other night," the PBN (Pretty Birdie Network) anchor said to the camera before playing the clip that had by then been seen millions of times. "The now-disgraced comedian has agreed to take some time away from the spotlight in order to focus on 'making himself better.' As discouraging as this type of behavior is, and with more reports of similar allegations starting to stack up against celebrities of all sorts, YZ's question is actually quite valid. How does the president manage to get away with things that for everyone else are societal taboos, and in some cases, even career-enders?

"All of this, of course, coming on the heel of former porn star Briana Gifford's claim that the president solicited her for sex when she was a minor. An allegation itself that came merely twenty-four hours before the ultimate passing of the Good to Go bill into law. No word yet on exactly when this new law is expected to go into effect, but things are certainly starting to get complicated, and one has to imagine the president is feeling the heat from both sides."

The broadcasting team at the Alpha Beta Network was also conducting their news show with a related segment of their own.

"Reports are coming in this afternoon of sexual harassment claims against radio and television personality Bryan Seachest," the Alpha Beta anchor said, "as well as pop star Dick Starter, who is, of course, a member of popular boy band, the Sidestreet Dudes."

Images of Seachest and Starter appeared on screen while the anchor continued.

"A young lady by the name of Kelly Swack has recently come forward with a story about how Starter got her pregnant when she was just fifteen years old. Here's the tearful interview she gave to one of our correspondents."

A pre-recorded clip of an interview with Kelly Swack began to play.

"I was a lifelong fan of the Sidestreet Dudes and I remember my parents got me backstage passes to one of their shows years ago for my fifteenth birthday," Kelly recalled, trying hard to hold back her tears. "Dick Starter was always my favorite. He struck me as such a nice guy and I thought he was so cute. I was thrilled when me and a friend got the chance to meet him. He took us to his private dressing room, which I thought was so cool, but by the time we left that room he had literally taken everything from both of us. Now I have a daughter who he's never seen, and he refuses to do anything to help raise her.

"Dick Starter is a monster! And the worst part is, the rest of his band, his agent, and the group's manager all know what happened but they don't care! They're covering it up and denying everything because they don't want it to ruin the group's squeaky-clean reputation! They have a rapist in their midst and they choose to do nothing about it. I make sure to boycott every Sidestreet Dudes performance now, and I encourage others to do the same."

The camera cut back to the Alpha Beta anchor.

"We were also able to speak to Kelly's friend, who corroborated the story," the anchor said before playing another clip.

"I'll never forget that night," another young woman, who identified herself as Jeanine Harlot, said. "I was so excited to go with my best friend on her birthday to see our favorite band, and I was extra stoked because her parents scored us backstage passes. Dick Starter met us alone after the show, which we didn't think anything of at the time, and he started out being so nice and super sweet, but the second we were in his dressing room, he changed. It was like a totally different person appeared.

"He had a lustful look in his eyes and he immediately began to strip. Kelly was too stunned to move, but I went to run and he grabbed me and tied me to a chair. He told me to enjoy the show because I would be next."

Jeanine paused and began to tear up. It was clearly difficult for her to relive this moment from her past.

"There's no need to go into graphic details, but I later found out I was pregnant, too. I went to a clinic and got an abortion behind my parents' back because I knew they'd kill me if they found out. How could I tell them a famous singer had raped me? They were more likely to think I'd been promiscuous with another boy my age. I shudder to think how many young women he's taken advantage of since."

The camera again cut back to the Alpha Beta anchor.

"Allegations against Seachest are particularly disturbing since former adult-entertainment star Briana Gifford chose Seachest's show as a vehicle for her own story regarding the president paying her for sex at the age of seventeen. Seachest thanked her for being brave enough to come forward with her story and even had the gall to go on record himself chastising that kind of behavior. His accuser, a former assistant by the name of Erica Sudds, has come forward with a story of her own."

A clip of Erica Sudds began to play.

"Not only was I a personal assistant to Bryan for three years, but he had just offered me the position of co-host on his radio show and even presented me with a contract that I had already signed when he tore it up in front of me for refusing to carry on an affair with him. I'm not going to be one of those women that tells you a sob story. Yes, I purposely slept with my boss for personal gain. But the minute he found out the sex was temporary, I was gone. That speaks volumes about the type of person he is, and it's something his current and future employees should be aware of."

The Alpha Beta anchor appeared once more.

"With all of these allegations popping up of powerful men taking advantage of women in seemingly subservient positions to them, one has to wonder how many more are out there, and what can we do as a society to make it stop?"

BNN, the Biased News network, a personal favorite of the president for its frequent favorable coverage of him, chose to air a related segment as well, albeit from a different perspective.

"There's apparently such a large group of these women coming forward now that the hashtag #AndMe is trending on social media," the BNN anchor said. "And you really have to ask yourself about the timing of all of this. Do we really have an entire population of women who have been abused by their superiors, or is it all a major conspiracy against the president with the recent passing of the 'Good to Go' law? I mean, look at the evidence here. Nothing about sexual harassment - zip, nada - until the president proposes this bill. Then said bill quickly becomes unpopular given the weight of the topic, and suddenly it's all, 'He touched me here,' and, 'I was a victim.' Call me a pessimist if you want, but the whole thing seems a little too convenient for me."

She's right, Veronica thought to herself as she watched the BNN broadcast at home on the computer she shared with her boyfriend. *That woman anchor is absolutely right. All these accusers coming out of nowhere lately does seem awfully convenient. I hate to dismiss these women's allegations as trivial, but even if every single one of them is telling the truth, that doesn't mean there won't be some who lie just to get their fifteen minutes of fame.*

Veronica finished watching the video and logged into a shared e-mail account she and Jake used for acting-related correspondence. She was disappointed to find the inbox was full of messages for her boyfriend but nothing for her.

Really? I've been sending out a ton of head shots and resumes all week and nothing? At least one of us seems to be doing well. What's your secret, Jake? What are you doing that I'm not?

She opened one of the newer messages out of curiosity and was surprised to see it was from a casting agent for R&B singer M. Belly's latest music video.

An offer to be in a music video for M. Belly? Holy shit!

Scrolling through the message, she found a mention of herself at the bottom and read it aloud.

"You are welcome, if you'd like, to bring along your girlfriend. I can't promise anything, but I may be able to find a spot for her on set depending on how many young ladies we end up casting for the shoot."

Veronica excitedly called for her boyfriend.

"Jake! When were you going to tell me about this?"

Jake suddenly appeared out of the bathroom wearing only shorts, with shaving cream on his face and a razor in hand.

"Tell you about what?" he asked.

"This e-mail you got from one of the casting agents for an M. Belly music video."

"They got back to me? That's so cool!" he said, just before realizing his girlfriend was snooping. "Wait a minute! What are you doing reading my mail?"

"Your mail? This is our collective e-mail account, remember?"

"True, but you still clicked on a message addressed to me. Why?"

"Is it against the law to take an interest in my boyfriend's career?

"No, but is it likewise against the law to have to wait until I tell you about these things myself?"

"Actually, yes. Yes it is. Glad you asked?"

"You're lucky I know you as well as I do, Veronica," Jake said, heading back to the bathroom to finish shaving. "Not everybody would be able to deal with your...idiosyncrasies."

Damn, he sure has a lot of people interested in him, Veronica thought to herself again when she was left alone in front of the computer once more. *I'm only human, so admittedly, I'm a bit jealous. And what that one anchor said about potentially fake accusers makes me wonder...No, I couldn't do that. He's my boyfriend. His success is my success. Right?*

Jake reemerged, now clean-shaven, and headed for the closet to change into his work clothes.

"You know, Veronica, I was thinking about it, and even though we do have a lot of shared accounts, I still would rather you not read my mail before I do. It's partly a matter of trust, but it's also a matter of when I check for messages, the newest ones will be bold, so they'll get my attention first. Unless you specifically remember to mark each message you open as unread, it's possible those are messages I won't see, and I don't like that."

"Okay, I get it. Sorry," Veronica apologized. "But can you

honestly tell me you've never opened my mail?"

"Yes, I can. I only open messages with my name on them, and my name isn't Veronica, just like yours isn't Jake."

"Fine, I yield. It won't happen again."

"Thank you."

Jake finished getting dressed and was about to leave the tiny space they called home, but wanted to end the conversation on a positive note with some words of encouragement for Veronica.

"Hey, don't sweat my landing more roles than you. You might be in a bit of a slump right now, but you'll pull through."

"You think so?"

"Yeah, I know so," he said, kissing her goodbye and heading out the door.

Veronica returned her attention back to the computer screen after he left, where the M. Belly e-mail was still open, and hit "reply."

Sorry, Jake, but I've got an agenda here. And even though it'll be hard to convince you otherwise, I promise it's not too personal.

Chapter 9

LIFE WAS STARTING TO be slightly less good for Bryan Seachest. Within days of the Briana Gifford interview he thought for sure would prove to be a bombshell and serve as the reveal of the year, he found out his former assistant, Erica Sudds, went public with their own affair, leaving a distaste in people's mouths when it came to hearing his name and turning his Hollywood Golden Boy status more Bronze. Who did Erica think she was airing his laundry out for everyone to see? Seachest believed that, similar to Vegas, what happened in someone's pants should stay in someone's pants, and he wasn't pleased that his reputation was becoming questionable. What happened to "innocent until proven guilty?" Yes, he was guilty, but the public didn't necessarily know that for a fact. And quite frankly, it wasn't any of their damn business!

That's why today's broadcast of his radio show was going to be so important. He had invited his friend, fellow pretty boy and pop star Dick Starter to the studio so the two of them could each address the allegations against them and explain their side of the story to hopefully clear their names. Seachest and Starter went so far back, they were practically in diapers together. They met at a daycare center when they were about four years old, and Seachest, who possessed an excellent memory, recalled the scene to himself like it was yesterday.

I had just been dropped off by my mother to this place for the first time, where she claimed I'd have the opportunity to play games and make lots of friends. The building was called, 'Yummy Baby Daycare Center.' I don't know where the name came from or why they thought it was a good idea, but I remember the sign with the name on it in different-colored letters and being greeted by something so colorful somehow made me feel relaxed and less anxious than when I first got out of my mom's car. I remember thinking after seeing the sign that maybe I would enjoy myself there after all. I walked into the building as Mom waved goodbye and the first thing I noticed was another kid, about my age, sitting in front of a pile of building blocks and pouting. Everyone else in the room seemed to be having fun, laughing and shouting as there were games of Tag, Pin the Tail on the Donkey, and Duck, Duck, Goose going on. Whatever drove me to do it, I walked straight toward the kid who wasn't enjoying himself and sat down next to him.

"What's your name?" I asked him.

"Dick," he said abruptly, not looking at me and choosing instead to stare straight ahead. He answered me so harshly, I thought he was insulting me rather than answering my question.

"Hey, I'm just trying to be nice. You're the only one here not smiling and laughing like everyone else. I thought maybe you could use a friend. You don't have to call me names. That wasn't nice."

"Huh?" he asked, finally looking at me and giving me his attention.

"You called me a bad name and I don't think that was very nice. Take it back."

"What are you talking about? You asked me for my name. It's Dick."

"Oh." I felt like an idiot, but I also started laughing.

"What's so funny?"

"When you said your name, you sounded so mad I thought you were calling me a dick. But it turns out you were just answering the question I asked you."

He started laughing too after that and then we were both laughing together.

"You're funny," he said, starting to take a liking to me. "What's your name?"

"Bryan."

"Cool. Thanks for cheering me up, Bryan. I've had a really frustrating day."

"Why? What's wrong?"

"You see these building blocks here?" Dick asked, gesturing to the pile of blocks in front of him.

"What about them?"

"I got them from a box that says you can use them to build anything you want. So I thought it would be neat to build one of those big cars that you can drive around in and go all around the room with it. But these stupid things are just a bunch of squares! There's no way I can build a car with them!"

I tried to hold it back but I couldn't help it and wound up laughing out loud again.

"What's so funny now?" Dick asked, a confused look on his face.

"You are," I said.

"How so?"

"Dude! You can't build a car out of these. They're mostly squares, just like you mentioned."

"But the box said I could build anything!"

"Yeah, anything that fits the shape of the blocks."

He paused for a second as it dawned on him how stupid he sounded. "Oh."

"Is that why you were so upset when I first saw you?"

"Yeah, but what you're saying kind of makes sense. I guess I should have known better."

We both laughed again.

"You're an okay kid," I said. "Even if your name is Dick."

"I'd rather be a Dick than a Bryan."

"Why?"

"Because Bryan be cryin' as he got mauled by a lion!"

I let what he said sink in for a second.

"I don't know if you meant that as an insult or not, but that's actually a pretty good rhyme!" I told him.

"No, I was just messing with you. And thanks! I've been told I have a knack that might be a bit whack but I just can't take it back."

"Dude! Are you in like, advanced classes or something?"

"Nah, man. I just have this way with words. I think when I grow up I want to be a songwriter."

"So you don't ever want to make any money? That's cool."

"Very funny," he said.

"I don't know about you, Dick, but my mom said I'm going to be coming here every day during the summer while she's at work. Are you going to be here a lot during the summer, too?"

"Probably. And you know what? It's not even because either of my parents have jobs and they need someone to watch me while they're at work. My dad takes the time while I'm here to 'pork my mom,' is what he told me."

"Your dad takes you to a daycare center so he can eat pork with your mom?"

"No, I don't think it's that, exactly, but it definitely has something to do with he and my mom wanting to be alone," Dick replied.

"Well, whatever the reason, we can hang out whenever we're here. I'm glad we met!"

"Me too!"

And that was that. The two of them became fast friends and had been part of each other's lives ever since. Now, as they sat in Seachest's studio, they had the chance to clear the air about the allegations both of them were facing and Seachest was looking forward to getting started.

"You ready?" Seachest asked his friend.

"Let's do this, bro," Starter responded.

The audio mixer was turned up, the broadcast button was on, and the words "On-Air" above the doorway were illuminated in neon red, indicating it was showtime.

"Good afternoon, everyone! You're taking over with Bryan Seachest, and I'm joined today by pop star and Sidestreet Dudes member Dick Starter, who's here to talk about his band's new album and upcoming tour as well as address these allegations about him that have recently come to light. Dick, thanks for being here."

"My pleasure. Thanks for having me, Bryan. There's obviously some things that need to be said but not a whole lot of people are willing to hear me out, so I appreciate this opportunity."

"Of course. Now for those of you who may be unaware of the matter, here's some brief background. Dick here, as well as myself, have both recently been accused of some pretty terrible things, and I, for one, am saddened by the thought that so many people are taking rumor and speculation as fact and refusing to see it for anything other than what it is, which is obviously a lie."

"It's crazy, man," Dick said. "These allegations are so out of character for us that I can't believe it's even an issue. But unfortunately, everyone in my camp is telling me I need to speak out, so here I am."

"So let's get right down to it, then. Do you even know who these girls are, or can you recall the night in question they're talking about?"

"Look, the Sidestreet Dudes have been together for over twenty years now. We've done a lot of touring throughout that time; we're gearing up for a tour right now as you mentioned earlier, and we meet with a ton of fans everywhere we go. Unless I'm in constant contact with someone or seeing the same people night after night, which is rare outside of my immediate bandmates, the expectation that I'd be able to pick someone out of a crowd and be like, 'Yeah, I totally remember you,' is a little unfair."

"So are you saying you've never met these girls?" Seachest asked.

"I'm saying something that apparently happened so long ago, unless it held some sort of significance for me personally, is hard to conjure up. That doesn't mean I've never met these girls. We don't do it so much anymore, but during our earlier years we offered backstage passes for an extra fee, and we would all take turns showing people around backstage, giving them a tour of our dressing rooms, letting them check out the tour bus, taking pictures with them - things like that. But the backstage passes never included one-night stands, and they certainly never included rape!"

"These girls, Kelly Swack and Jeanine Harlot, are all over the media saying you forced yourself on them. One of them even claims she's raising your daughter. What's your response to that?"

"Well, I'm certainly not about to admit it, if that's what you're asking. There's nothing to admit to. Again, have I taken fans backstage in the past? Yes. Have some of them been alone with me in my dressing room? Yes. But if the question everyone wants an answer to is, 'Have I ever slept with and impregnated underage girls?' The answer is unequivocally, no! And I want this to be the last I have to say on the matter, because it's starting to get out of hand."

"I have to agree with you on that," Seachest said. "Take my situation, for example. Erica Sudds, who, as I'm sure everyone has heard by now, used to be a personal assistant of mine, has been making her way around the media as well with outrageous claims that I fired her when she refused to sleep with me. Now, I'm not going to sit here and proclaim to be perfect. I think any time two attractive people work together there's going to be some temptation for a little inter-office romance. Admittedly, I've had quite a few eligible young ladies work for me in the past. I was actually even engaged to one for a while.

"Long-time listeners probably remember one of my former co-hosts, Briana Huss. We were both very upfront with the public about our relationship, which proved to be a double-edged sword, because a public engagement also means a public falling out when things go south, and that is one relationship that obviously didn't go as planned. She went to our producers and asked for a raise, thought I had something to do with it when they told her no, even though I had no idea she felt she was being cheated in terms of her pay, and everything spiraled out of control from there."

"I remember that," Starter said, chuckling. "She created a media circus of her own by crowning you as the King of Misogyny and an opponent of women's rights."

"That she did," Seachest said, chuckling as well. "But I only bring that up as a way to say I'm always the first to admit my flaws. And while I can't recall why the producers held out on Briana or why she was claiming the things she was claiming, it's important to me people know that if there was something to talk about, I would talk about it. Erica's on the verge of being happily married herself, from what I understand, so what she thinks she stands to gain by creating a false narrative, I couldn't begin to guess."

"She's obviously trying to ruin your career."

"I have had a few long-time collaborators recently cut ties with me, I'm sorry to say. But I'd like to think in the end, the truth always prevails. People know me. I don't mean to brag by saying this, but I'm literally everywhere. After this show, I'm off to host the popular reality competition, *Glorified Karaoke*, I fly to New York five days a week to co-host *Live! With Bryan & Shelly*, I produce another popular reality series, *Keeping Up For No Reason*, I'm the face of New Year's Eve! Forgive me, Dick, but even with your extensive recording and touring schedule, I think I stay busier than you do."

"No argument here, brother," Starter agreed.

"All of this is just to say that if I slept with every disgruntled female colleague who claims she had an affair with me, I wouldn't have half as many credits to my name because I'd be burning too many bridges."

"And didn't you also have Briana Gifford on earlier in the week to tell her story?"

"Yes, I did. And thank you for mentioning that because I think that just further proves my point. Why would I have a victim of sexual harassment on the show if doing so could potentially expose me to a sexual harassment allegation of my own? I don't want to keep rambling on and on about the same thing, but I do think it warrants repeating. Whatever reason Erica Sudds chose to leave my employ, it had absolutely nothing to do with us sleeping together! And as you said, Dick, with this, I hope I can rest my case."

"Amen, bro," Starter said. "Now if you don't mind, I'm going to switch gears. In addition to addressing the allegations, the guys also wanted me to talk about our new album."

"Oh, yes. Of course. Sometimes it's easy to forget my guests have projects to promote and don't just come to pay social calls."

"Don't get me wrong, Bryan. We can totally hang out after the show if you'd like, but the Sidestreet Dudes are releasing our first album of new material in five years. It's kind of a big deal."

"Wow, five years? Has it really been that long?"

"I know. We have trouble believing it too, sometimes, but yeah, it has. Main Roads Are For Sissies came out five years ago to the day that Gotta Love Shortcuts is going to be released."

"I love both of those as album titles, by the way, Dick. Very clever marketing."

"Thank you."

"So let's talk about the new tunes. How do you think the group's songwriting style has changed between this album and the last?"

"Well, you know, we're big believers in the mantra, 'If it's not broken, don't fix it,' so to be honest, I think our overall musical style is very much the same..."

Best friends Kelly Swack and Jeanine Harlot, the victims of Dick Starter who'd recently gone public with their allegations, were in Kelly's living room listening to Seachest and Starter blatantly lie about their behavior on Seachest's radio show, when Kelly decided she couldn't take it anymore and got up to turn the radio off, outraged.

"Can you believe these two?" Kelly angrily asked her friend. "The complete and utter lack of respect they're showing by making light of their situations is repulsive! And did you hear what Dick said about the night he met us? 'Unless it holds significance to me it's hard to conjure up.' That's such bullshit! He knocked us both up and he's passing it off as nothing!"

"I know. Believe me, Kel, I'm just as frustrated as you are. But we appear to be very tiny minnows swimming in a very vast body of water. If people refuse to separate celebrities from their public personas, there's not much we can do about it."

"I can't accept that! We were taken advantage of, damn it! I have an eight-year-old on the other side of the fucking house sleeping because she needs to get up early for school tomorrow! Where did that child come from, huh? Does everybody think I just magically made her appear?"

"They're saying we have no credibility because we waited so long to tell our stories," Jeanine explained to Kelly. "Apparently we're gold-diggers who have nothing better to do than tell lies in an effort to exploit the rich and powerful for cash."

"But that's not true!"

"You and I know it isn't, but convincing the public at large is proving to be pretty difficult."

"So you're just going to give up?"

"What do you want me to tell you, Kel? That I want to continue to be ridiculed when it's hurtful enough to open up wounds from the past? I only went public with my own account of that night because I thought it would help to back up yours. I thought if two women came forward with the exact same story, they wouldn't be able to ignore both of us. I was obviously wrong. They don't care. Nobody does. And as much as being recognized for telling the truth and seeing Dick Starter brought to justice would be nice, I don't want to be known the rest of my life as the girl who cried rape. I'm sorry. We tried."

"That's easy for you to say!" Kelly shouted. "You don't have a permanent souvenir from that night that's totally dependent on you 24/7!"

"I could have!"

"But you don't! I didn't have the luxury of aborting my problem, Jeannie! Don't get me wrong, I love my daughter, but it's increasingly hard for me to live with the fact I have real, child-sized proof of that bastard's crimes and nobody will believe me!"

Jeanine looked away from Kelly with hurt in her eyes.

"You think getting that abortion was a luxury?" she said, holding back tears. "Do you have any idea how hard it was to walk up to the Planned Parenthood clinic with all those crazy, right-wing freaks outside, with their shouts of, 'Murderer!' and 'Baby Killer!' making me feel like I was the bad guy?"

Kelly put her hand on Jeanine's shoulder in an effort to console her.

"I'm sorry, Jeannie. I didn't mean it like that."

"I know. But I can't keep fighting like this, Kel. When it gets to a point where no matter what you do or don't do people aren't going to believe you, and that's clearly where we're at with this, then it's kind of hard to see the point, you know? Why keep shouting over a bunch of unruly, uneducated idiots?"

"Because if you shout loud enough, someone's bound to hear you eventually," Kelly replied. "Forget about doing this for us. Do it for those who have yet to be victimized. If the two of us together can prevent just one young girl from idolizing the wrong person, then that's at least one less incident in the world. Isn't that worth fighting for?"

"Nobody should have to deal with what we did," Jeanine said, finally giving in to her tears and wiping them from her eyes.

"Then don't give up! I need you with me on this, Jeannie. There's a group of people somewhere out there who will listen. And I'm equally sure there's a woman out there just like us who will give voice to the cause."

"Oh, yeah? Who?"

"I don't know yet. But she's out there. She's got to be."

Jake had just pulled into the parking lot of the restaurant he worked at when his cellphone rang. Since he was a few minutes early, he decided to take the call.

"Hello?"

"Hi, I'm looking to speak to Jake Asworth."

"This is he."

"Jake, this is Stonewall Price. I'm one of the producers working on the M.Belly music video."

"Oh, hi, Mr. Price!" Jake greeted his caller, surprised with whom he was speaking. "I'm actually headed into work. Would you mind if I called you back later tonight or tomorrow?"

"Not to be a prick, kid, but I'm actually on set prepping for the shoot which is scheduled to take place soon. Why the hell are you where are you instead of here where I am?"

Jake was confused by the question.

"I'm sorry, sir, I'm afraid I don't understand."

"What's there to understand?" Price snarled, annoyed. "You sent me an e-mail earlier accepting the role and I sent you one back with all the details, including when to be here. Did you not get it?"

"I'm sorry, sir. I think there's been a mistake. I didn't send..."

Jake's voice trailed off for a second as he thought back to his conversation with the one person who would do something like that behind his back.

"Veronica!" he blurted out.

"Your girlfriend?" Price asked. "Yeah, she's already here. One of the other female extras admitted she wasn't comfortable having to give Belly a lap dance so I found a spot for her after all. She got lucky."

"Yeah. Lucky."

"So are you on your way or not? You seem like a nice kid and all, but I'm not about to hold things up for someone who's not the main attraction. No offense."

"None taken. I'll head there now. Anything specific I should wear?"

"Christ, kid!" Price said. "I told you all that information is in the e-mail!"

"Sorry, sir, but that's apparently a message I didn't get to see."

"Listen, just get here, okay? We'll throw you to wardrobe and get you on set. Sound good?"

"Sounds great!"

"Beautiful! You've got twenty minutes before cameras roll. If you're late, we're not going to use you. Got it?"

"Got it."

"Great! See you, kid!"

Jake ended the call and put his phone back in his pocket. He sat in his car in the parking lot for a moment, staring at the building that had been a second home to him over the last few years. If he bailed on his shift, he knew that would be it. He had made great money there and the job, though sometimes stressful, wasn't overly difficult, but management was unforgiving, and would only remember him for the last thing he did. In this case, that last thing was going to be as a no-call, no-show.

"I hope you realize you just cost me my job, Veronica," Jake said aloud to himself, as he started his car's engine and headed to the video shoot. "You better have a damn good explanation for this."

THERE WERE ROUGHLY A dozen extras hanging around the set of the video. To nobody's surprise, they were all female, all young, and all very impressionable. For some, this was their first time in front of the camera working on a professional shoot. For others, they'd not only had a hefty resume as background actors, but started to develop personal relationships with the production's star, M. Belly, as Belly tended to grow fond of those who worked for him in the past and would reuse the same girls as human props over and over again.

The set itself was made up to look like a beach, albeit a very cheap one. There was a scant amount of sand, a couple of inflatable beach balls, and some pails and shovels lying around. Belly himself sat on a plastic chair in the middle of the room, dressed as a lifeguard. He couldn't help but scan his surroundings and admire the attire of the young extras, imagining what he wanted to do to some after the shoot was over while he had the others film so he could archive the activities and store them for future viewings as proof of his appeal to the pre-teen and teen generation.

Although his personal choices could be seen as questionable, Belly made sure he was extremely efficient and methodical when it came to his professional life. He prided himself on starting a project on time and never settled for anything less than perfection when it came to his work and with those whom he chose to collaborate. Therefore, he was less than thrilled when the shoot that was supposed to have started nearly a half-hour ago still had yet to commence, the director was nowhere to be found, and Stonewall Price, one of the producers that Belly took on as a sympathy hire because he had heard of his sporadic work history and felt sorry for him, was throwing his weight around the set, feeling it necessary to shout orders to anyone and everyone in sight.

"Okay, people!" Price shouted to the assembled background actors. "Split the room! Let's get half of the extras on one side and half on the other! I want a handful of girls surrounding Belly, and I want that Veronica chick on the floor in front of him, ready to leap up and give him a lap dance as soon as she gets the signal!"

Belly had had enough.

"What's your problem, brother?" Belly asked Price. "You aren't the director!"

"As of about ten minutes ago, I am now. The director never showed and I'm the only other behind-the-scenes guy here, so I was given the green light by the studio to start calling the shots."

"For reals?" Belly asked again, clearly perplexed. "Damn, ain't that a bitch!"

"You're telling me. I didn't ask for this! I was hired to handle logistics: help with casting, making sure this thing stays within budget, that kind of thing. But don't worry, I have experience."

"I know what you were brought on for, brother. I'm on the one responsible for taking a chance on your ass. Now, let's talk about this so-called 'experience' you have. What other artists have you done videos for that I might have seen?"

"Well," Price replied, looking sheepish. "It was actually a thirty-second voyeuristic clip of my sister in the shower that was done when I was kid, but it was a video, and she sang to actual music, so that's got to count for something."

Belly shook his head.

"If I wasn't so embarrassed for you, I'd throw your ass out of here. But you're still the producer, and we apparently need a director, so just don't fuck this up, 'aight?"

"Come on! It's a video for a song by you. How much more could I fuck it up?"

Belly didn't like that comment. In his mind, he wasn't just a singer, he was a bona fide artiste. Born with true God-given talent, it was his purpose and responsibility in life to share that talent with the world. His songs weren't just songs, they were monologues set to a drum track that revealed pieces of his soul - beautiful masterpieces of lyricism that gave voice to the world society dealt with on a daily basis. Without him, R&B as the expressive and representative genre it was simply wouldn't exist. Angelic harmonies on hits like "Can't Find My Sock," "Staring at the Sky Part Thirty-One," and "You're Too Old For Me" set a new bar for musical genius everywhere. How dare Price suggest a video for one of his tunes could be anything less than amazing!

"What the fuck is that supposed to mean?" Belly asked angrily, as he stood up and got in Price's face.

"I didn't mean anything by it, Belly," Price said, hands up in a defensive gesture. "I was joking. That's all it was. Just a joke."

"Well keep your jokes to your damn self and get behind that camera!" Belly said, as he headed back to his chair. "Let's make us a..." he paused, remembering Price's words from earlier. "...video with music."

Jake finally arrived on set just as Price was prepping the camera and about to call for action.

"Jake! Christ, kid! I said if you were late we wouldn't use you! This is what I consider late!"

"Sorry, sir. I ran into traffic and parking was a little difficult."

"What do you mean? There's parking right out front. All you had to do was give your keys to the valet and tell him you're a part of the M. Belly shoot."

"There was no valet when I got here," Jake said. "All I saw was a sign down the street that said '$20 Parking,' so that's where I parked."

"Well, I hope for your sake your car's still there when you're done here. Hurry over to wardrobe and makeup and you might still have a chance of being on screen, but I make no promises."

"Thank you, sir."

Jake headed to HMU (hair and makeup) when he heard Veronica call out to him.

"Jake!" his girlfriend shouted.

"Veronica," Jake acknowledged her. "You owe me a serious explanation as to what we're both doing here right now, but we can worry about that later."

"Explanation?" Veronica asked, feigning confusion. "You're the one who owes me an explanation! You said you were going to keep your distance from me for a while!"

"What? What are you talking about?"

"Hey, let's save the lover's quarrel for later, okay?" Price said, cutting into their conversation. "You two want to be a part of this thing or not?"

"Mr. Price, I can't work with this man!" Veronica said, pointing to Jake.

"Why the fuck not?" Price asked. "I thought he was your boyfriend!"

"He's no boyfriend of mine. That man you just allowed onto your set is a rapist!"

The room suddenly became abuzz with confusion and speculation. M. Belly didn't care for the delay and tried to take charge of the situation.

"Can we get this thing on film today, please?" Belly called out. "I have some...commitments to tend to later."

"I bet you do!" shouted a female voice from backstage. Everybody turned toward the direction of the voice to see to whom it belonged. Belly was surprised when he realized he recognized the speaker. It was one of his cousins, a young lady by the name of Aisha Fillmore.

Aisha and Belly shared a special history together that went way beyond familial relations. Aisha had come to temporarily live with Belly and his parents when the two of them were younger. She was fourteen and he was twenty-two at the time. Being that Belly had always had a thing for younger girls, he thought his cousin was particularly attractive and went out of his way to treat her like a queen - buying her whatever she wanted, constantly complimenting her looks, taking her out to restaurants, movies, and other social events, and generally doing his best to flirt with her. She didn't have a boyfriend at the time and absolutely loved the attention. It didn't take long before the two were unofficially dating and Belly found his way into her pants. Aisha genuinely believed she was in love but to her cousin, it was nothing more than a fling, lasting only as long as she lived with them and ending as soon as he met someone he found even younger and more attractive than her. From that moment on, she made it a personal goal of hers to expose the singer for the kind of man he really was.

"Aisha, baby!" Belly greeted her. "Why didn't you tell me you were gonna be on set? I could have bumped you up to something much more important than just an extra!"

"I don't want to be any closer to you than I have to be!" Aisha shouted. "In fact, I'm here to sabotage this video! Sorry, everyone, but you should know that M. Belly is also a rapist!"

Nobody reacted to Aisha's comment, so she tried again.

"Didn't you all hear me? M. Belly is a rapist! He sleeps with teenage girls, marries teenage girls, and all around him, almost every second of every day is nothing but teenage girls!"

When an awkward moment of silence went by with still nobody seeming to care about Aisha's "revelation," Price interjected and broke the ice.

"Sorry. Aisha, was it? If your only intention is to interfere then you're going to have to leave. These trivial back-and-forths are putting us way behind schedule."

"'Trivial back-and-forths?'" Aisha cried, surprised nobody around her was taking her claim more seriously. "My cousin, right over there," she said, pointing to Belly, "has bedded minors throughout his entire career. I know because I was one of them. Doesn't that bother anybody?"

Still no reaction from anyone, suggesting they weren't bothered at all.

"I'm afraid that's not a secret, dear," Price said. "We're all well-aware of Belly's preference for young blood, we just don't care because we happen to find the man highly entertaining, however odd his behavior might be."

"I can't argue with that," Belly agreed. "I am pretty fucking weird."

"Seriously?" Aisha couldn't believe what she was hearing. "Isn't there anybody in this room who cares that M. Belly has slept with more children than teddy bears?"

"Ah, come on! Don't be like that, cuz!" Belly said. "Just because we drifted apart as you got older doesn't mean we can't still be friends."

"'Friends?'" she cried. "I gave you my childhood, my teen years, even the first half of my twenties! And for what? I loved you! And even though you knew it was wrong you encouraged that love! Now I'm supposed to forget everything that happened and play nice? What the hell is wrong with you?"

"This is starting to get on my nerves," Price cut in. "I'm not sure what made you think this particular moment was the right time to air out your family's dirty laundry, but you need to leave now!"

"I can't believe this isn't bothering anybody!" Aisha said, looking around the room a final time for any empathy or sympathy from the crowd. "I really thought today would be the day I ended my cousin's career!"

"Well, evidently you were wrong, darling," Price said. "Look, I realize Belly is a disgusting man, as I think we all do."

"Again, I can't even argue with that," Belly declared.

"And maybe if someone made a documentary about it and broadcast it on national television," Price continued, "people would pay a bit more attention to his lifestyle and realize he needs some serious help, because that's how today's world works. But as of this moment in time, no such documentary exists, so please, if you would be so kind, GET THE FUCK OFF MY SET!" he yelled.

Stunned that everyone was so numb to her allegations, Aisha

stormed off the set without looking back. Veronica, meanwhile, was still looking to tarnish her boyfriend's reputation.

"Now that that's out of the way, can we get back to my revelation? That man," Veronica said, once again pointing at Jake, "forced himself on my best friend the other night and refuses to acknowledge it! Can we please have him leave too? Don't forget, I was the only girl willing to give M. Belly a lap dance on camera!"

"That's true," Belly said. "We went through like, fifteen bitches who all said 'Hell, nah!' before we got a 'Hell, yeah!'"

"Fine!" Price gave in, trying to keep his cool. "Jake, I'm sorry, but I have to ask you to leave."

"What?" Jake cried. "Veronica, where did you hear that? And what makes you think I would actually do that? Courtney's my friend, too!"

"I don't want to talk to him, Mr. Price," Veronica said, turning away from Jake and refusing to look at him. "Please?"

"Get out of here, kid!" Price said. "It's nothing personal."

"But I walked away from my job for this role!" Jake shouted.

Veronica cringed inwardly when she heard him say that and felt a brief pang of guilt, but it was gone as soon as it came.

"Jake, we're already so far behind here," Price said. "If you don't leave right now, I'm going to throw you out personally! Go!"

"Fine! I'm going!" Even though she wouldn't look at him, Jake turned to the person at one point he thought was his girlfriend before he left. "Don't even think of coming back to the apartment tonight, Veronica! I need some alone time so I can figure things out!"

Like Aisha before him, Jake also stormed off the set not looking back, while Price finally began to call things to order.

"Okay, enough distractions! Let's shoot a fucking music video, huh? Now remember, girls all around Belly as the song begins. Veronica, as soon as you see one of the beach balls land in front of you, jump on our star here and get that lap dance going. Everybody ready? And...ACTION!"

<u>**Chapter 11**</u>

DILL MOSEBY WAS A name everyone knew. It seemed
regardless of one's background and personal tastes, just about all who
heard of him agreed he was a living legend in the comedy community with
major star power. Even now, over forty years into his career, he continued
to tour throughout the world to massive audiences and sold-out venues
wherever he went. He'd always had moderate success as a stand-up comic,
but his breakout role came when he received the opportunity to headline
his own primetime sitcom, aptly titled, *The Moseby Show*. He was in his
mid-forties at the time and had been grinding away at the comedy club
circuit for about a decade. Moseby enjoyed life on the road, getting to
travel to places he'd never been, playing tourist when he wasn't
performing, and of course, he found the women everywhere he went to be
top-notch. Some of them were easier to get into his bed than others, but
the ones who proved a little more...challenging, just required a different

approach, usually of the "Why don't you take this so you can relax?" kind. But in his mind that didn't make him a bad person, just an aggressive one.

As fun as stand-up was, though, when an executive from WTF, the Way Too Funny Network, met him backstage after one his shows at a venue in Los Angeles one night, and said he wanted to explore the possibility of using him in a sitcom and adapt some of his material for television, Moseby couldn't say no. He met with the head of WTF's programming a week later and the seeds got planted for what later become the number one show in America. If he thought notoriety from his live performances was a rush, the nearly instant fame that came from being on live TV hit him like a hardcore drug.

No wonder some celebrities had such massive egos! Dill Moseby suddenly found himself recognized everywhere he went, be it restaurants, grocery stores, or taking a walk around his own neighborhood. There was even a time he called a computer company to ask an IT guy a question about his laptop's specs, and the man on the other end freaked out when he realized who was calling. It didn't hurt that his sitcom happened to prove historic for the network it ran on either. *The Moseby Show* was about an all-black family, therefore featuring an all-black cast in the lead roles, and was a hit among multiple generations and races of fans. Moseby began noticing his live crowds contained people from all walks of life, and couldn't help but marvel at what a difference a simple tube with moving images could make for his career. Of course, he wasn't the first black man to lead a TV show; the '70s sitcoms, *What's Happening!!* and *The Jeffersons* came to mind, but he was the first one to be given a slot on WTF, a network infamous for filling its airwaves with white-washed "dramadies" and trashy reality shows, which was a big deal at the time.

When the show's ratings catapulted it to number-one and kept it there for almost the entirety of its eight-season run, Moseby knew he could have anything he wanted, and what he wanted was young, eager-to-please, aspiring starlets. These young ladies who got to meet him, whether at social events, networking functions, or otherwise, always asked him the same thing, "What advice do you have for people trying to break into the entertainment industry?" Or "Do you think you could put in a good word for me with (insert casting director's name here)?" His answer, likewise, was always the same: "Take down my number and we'll talk." In some cases, he would have chance encounters with these girls at places he was staying, which would change the reply to, "Come on up to my room with me and we'll talk about what exactly you want to do."

Playing a family patriarch on a nationally renowned TV show meant his reputation preceded him, at least the fictional one. Most of America knew him as the fatherly figure the scripts had him portray, so nobody who met him in real life would have ever guessed he was actually a sex addict and serial rapist. Why would they? There was nothing to suspect! He was a middle-aged man of African-American descent who was kind to all and generous with both his time and his money, giving back by donating a significant amount of his yearly earnings to charities helping black youths. He even served as a symbol to the community at large that if he could be successful, so could anybody; all it took was a little hard work, and maybe the right connections, which he could help provide.

So it stood to reason these young ladies, giddy with stars in their eyes having met one of their idols, would take Moseby up on his offer and call him for a personal chat, or follow him up to his hotel room for a potentially life-changing experience. As far as the latter, they were never disappointed. Whenever he got alone time with his female fans, he wined them, dined them and - depending on how receptive they were once his intentions were made known - made his move and let the chips fall where they may. Sometimes it was easy, other times not so much. But if there was one thing Moseby could say about that phase of his life, he was never lacking for company. Sure, he occasionally felt guilty about using his status as a Hollywood big-shot to get into women's pants, but if he didn't do it, somebody else would! And it's not like he had anything to be concerned about. On the off-chance one of his former conquests told anybody, they would think she was crazy and just looking for attention. He was America's Dad! No way would someone who had garnered such an image behave so despicably! Absolutely not!

All these years later, the aging comedian was less active between the sheets, but his touring schedule was just as demanding and he was as popular as ever. He had recently taken some time away from the spotlight as he got older, but he found even semi-retirement a bore and after expressing to his manager his desire to return to the stage, he once again became inundated with performances at venues across the country, which, to his great pleasure, were still largely selling out. Dill Moseby had stopped being merely a person throughout the years, and had become a brand, an icon, a name synonymous with comedy, to the point where as long as he was still doing what he did best, people would be there to watch.

It was late at night after one of his recent shows, a run of performances the media referred to as his "comeback tour," and Moseby was enjoying some deserved alone time in a hotel room, on the cusp of sleep, when his cellphone rang. He saw movie mogul Carver Spleensteen's name on the caller ID and rolled his eyes, considering ignoring the call. The phone rang several more times before he decided to go against his impulses and answer it.

"I'm on the east coast right now, Spleensteen, not in L.A. It's one o'clock in the morning over here. Whatever you have to say can wait until tomorrow. Let an old man sleep, why don't you?"

"Sorry, Dill, but Todd and I are a little on edge. Have you been paying attention to the news lately?"

"A beloved and renowned entertainer such as myself doesn't pay attention to news, he makes news. Why? What's going on?"

"A storm's coming, Dill," Spleensteen ominously replied. "And if we don't start being more careful, we're going to have some major problems."

"What the hell are you talking about, Spleensteen? Spit it out!"

"It's the women, Dill. They seem to be...revolting!"

Moseby couldn't help laughing.

"Are you kidding me? You're worried about women? Give me a fucking break!"

"I'm serious! All these idiots that have been thinking with their dicks their entire careers are starting to get called out for their behavior.

Seachest, Starter, YZ, Tiersen...their reputations are all unraveling as more and more women speak out on their misogyny and sexual threats. We're a part of those idiots, Dill! All it'll take is a bit of encouragement from some chick who's already gone to the media for some other chick to tell a story about us!"

Moseby stopped laughing.

"I agree the situation's a little bothersome, but of the two of us, you have more to worry about than I do."

"What makes you say that?" Spleensteen asked.

"I know you, son. When you audition these actresses for roles in your films, you don't even try to make your intentions a secret. Todd told me how you handled that Felicia...something or other."

"Donner. Her name is Felicia Donner."

"See? That's what I'm talking about! Not only do you approach her for sex in an unfiltered, cut-throat way, you remember her full name! You want to be a boss and get away with shit like me, you've gotta learn to deny, deny, deny."

"Fuck you! At least when I get pussy the girl's agreed to sleep with me while she's awake and aware of what's going on! I don't have to drug her and have my way with her under the radar like a certain coward I know!"

"You say potato, I say, 'Here, bitch, take these pills,'" Moseby said. "You can mock all you want but it works every time. Nearly four decades and counting."

"You're lucky, is what you are. Of all those aspiring actresses and models you've had a taste of throughout the years, I can't believe not a single one has woken up in an awkward position in the home of one of their idols and not wondered what the hell happened to them the previous night or how they got there."

"Oh, I'm sure they all have. Some of them have probably even connected the dots. But when it comes right down to it, they're keeping their mouths shut for two reasons. One, they're embarrassed and just want to put what few memories they have of the occasion out of their minds, never to be thought of again. And two, I'm Dill Fucking Moseby, an

American icon! If they even remotely considered going to the press and ratting me out, who do you think is more likely to be believed? Some skank who found herself in a skanky situation, or the man with the wholesome father figure image who just recently donated millions to a local charity?"

"Fair point," Spleensteen said.

"You're damn right, 'fair point!' Take a page or two out of my book, son. You might learn something."

"So to avoid a scandal, you're saying I need to stop propositioning my cast?"

"Hell, no! I'm saying you need to stop being so obvious about it! When I invite a young lady over, she has no idea what she's getting herself into, and that's how it should be. Her guard is down and she's not suspicious of anything. She may be a bit vulnerable being in such an intimate environment with someone that's practically a stranger, but I'm America's Dad! Therefore, she knows she's safe around me!"

"Ah, I get it. You use your public persona to your advantage."

"You learn quickly, my student."

"But my public persona is being a sleazeball! That's why I'm so worried! I feel like as soon as someone says something, everyone that's ever worked with me will be like, 'Well, no shit, Sherlock!'"

Spleensteen's comment made Moseby pause.

"If things are really starting to get as bad as you say," Moseby said after some thought, "I suggest you change your public persona, and fast. Maybe reach out to Felicia Whoever."

"Donner!"

"Whatever! Reach out to her and apologize. Tell her you know what you did was wrong. It couldn't hurt. Of course, that's something I would never do, but we're comparing apples to oranges."

"That's why I love you, Dill! I knew you'd steer me in the right direction!"

"It's a heavy burden for the one who knows all and is all, but when you have a gift for wisdom, you must dispense your knowledge."

"That was beautiful, man."

"Glad you think so. I'm developing a new TV series for the Pretty Birdie Network and I think that's one of the lines I want my character to be known for, so I wanted to try it out. Now, for fuck's sake, can I get some sleep?"

"Sure thing," Spleensteen said. "Sorry to bother you so late. Listen, I know you think you're untouchable, but make smart decisions, all right? If a ninja like you goes down, I have a feeling the rest of us will soon follow."

"I think that's a safe bet. I'm going to end the call now. If you're still talking when I do, that's your problem. I'll call you when I'm back in town. Night."

"Night, old man."

Moseby ended the call, put his phone on the dresser next to him, and smiled to himself as he lay in bed.

Man, even at this age, he thought to himself before drifting off to sleep, *it's still good to be King.*

In a New York comedy club that same night, a fellow comedian, Cannibal Duress, was about to change Dill Moseby's world forever, as he performed a set about the recent Hollywood sexual scandals and the #AndMe movement to a receptive audience. Though the crowd appeared to be enjoying themselves, what came out of Duress's mouth next shocked everyone in the room and put a permanent stain on Moseby's legacy.

"Forget about people like Bryan Seachest and Dick Starter for a second. You know who really has balls when it comes to taking what they want by any means? Dill Moseby! There's no stopping that guy!"

Duress paused as he waited for a reaction. His audience was clearly town between laughing and feeling uncomfortable. What could Dill Moseby have to do with what was happening with Bryan Seachest and Dick Starter? They were about to find out.

"Somehow, no one's come forward to say this yet, so for those afraid to ruffle feathers or stir a pot that's been settled for too long, I'll say it for them."

Another dramatic pause from Duress as the audience was on the edge of their seat. What was the performer about to say?

"You're a rapist, Dill Moseby!" Duress declared as the crowd gasped.

Everyone wondered how such an accusation could be true. More importantly, how did Cannibal Duress know what he was saying was indeed a fact?

"Moseby is the epitome of the ultimate sexual predator," Duress continued. "But then again, you don't have too many options when you're that age, do you?"

The audience started to relax and found themselves laughing again at the humor in imagining geriatric sex.

"I mean, on the one hand, you gotta give credit where credit's due, right? Here you have this old, black man, a fucking prune by anyone's standards, and not only does he somehow miraculously still manage to maintain an erection without medical assistance, his libido's as active as ever! I'll be happy if I'm half as sexually active as that dude when I'm his age. Damn!"

The audience was in hysterics, Duress having won back their support.

"And his technique is pretty slick. It takes the term 'human sex doll' to a whole new level. You see, Moseby's figured out the secret to guaranteed sex that the rest of us already know, but never bother to act on. A still body can't say no. Let's be realistic. An eighty-year-old man can't just mosey on up to a gorgeous-looking twenty-year-old and spit some game. For one thing, any line he's about to pull out of his playbook is at least fifty years old. No way in hell a college co-ed is going to wet herself over a reference from an era when she was still a streak of cum in her father's ball sack.

"And then there's the whole grandfather thing. If you do enough research, then maybe, just maybe, you might be able to find an example or two of a daughter hooking up with or fantasizing about her father. The term 'incest' exists for a reason. It's out there and it happens, no doubt. But

I'd bet money on the fact that you'd be pretty damn hard-pressed to find a sweet young thing that's constantly fantasizing or lusting after her grandfather. Show me an example of that and I'll pay you a thousand dollars, cash. I'm not saying it never happens, but granddaddy issues have got to be a hell of a lot more rare than daddy issues."

The audience's laughter increased in volume. They loved what they were hearing.

"But all of this is just to say, of course the dude has to drug women! Especially nowadays. I mean, I would never consciously sleep with an older lady who looks like she could keel over at any moment. However, if you drugged my ass, put me in a bed with her, and had her use my body to pleasure herself without my knowing, then she could do anything she wanted until I woke up.

"See the difference? In one situation, you strike out. In the other one, you win. So I get why Moseby did what he did. But it's wrong! Dill Moseby needs to stop this despicable behavior, and the women he's taken advantage of need to let him know they're not going to stand for it anymore!"

Duress bowed to the audience while they erupted in applause. However inadvertent it might have been, his performance had just set in motion a series of events that weren't only going to put the #AndMe movement under a bigger microscope, but would also result in victims finally coming forward, creating a domino effect that would change Hollywood forever.

Chapter 12

HELEN DEGENERATE WAS THE queen of daytime television and she knew it. That's not to say she was arrogant or had a superiority complex, but numbers don't lie, and her mid-afternoon talk show consistently ranked as number one in the country for that particular time slot. Most of her demographic was either stay-at-home moms, unemployed housewives, or women with sugar daddies who had nothing better to do than veg out in front of a TV all day since their every want and desire was tended to, courtesy of that magical paper called money. But none of that mattered. As long as people tuned in, the ratings remained solid and she was able to provide the illustrious lifestyle for her and her wife the two of them had grown accustomed to over the years.

Like most in her position, Helen got her start in stand-up as a teenager. Somebody eventually took notice, which led to the inevitable short-lived sitcom, which led to her dating one of the female crew members of said sitcom, which in turn led to her coming out publicly in the midst of production on the sitcom. Then, through various twists, turns and opportunities that only Hollywood could provide, she wound up with her own daytime talk show, which she had since hosted for the past decade. Her life had been a whirlwind, to be sure, but in a good way. She was one of those celebrities who enjoyed using her power for good and would sometimes dedicate entire episodes to certain themes or people whose stories begged to be told. Taking a page out of Oprah's book, she even had daily giveaways on her show, which always served as a nice little ego boost to remind both herself and her audience members that yes, she was rich, but they could still be fans of hers because everyone would reap the benefits.

Today was one of those shows she chose to dedicate to a particular cause; a situation she believed didn't get the spotlight as much as it deserved and certainly wasn't discussed enough in a public space. One of her producers was contacted earlier in the week by a trio of women, sisters who claimed they'd been abused by comedian Dill Moseby when they were younger, back when he was at the peak of his career and popularity. After keeping their experience to themselves for so long, they decided they were ready to talk about what happened and take their allegations public. As big fans of Helen's, they trusted her to handle their story with the elegance and tact it deserved, so got in touch with the show and asked if they could talk about everything on national television.

The producers and Helen were both skeptical at first. Why had the sisters waited so long to come forward? Was there sufficient evidence to back up their claims to avoid the show veering into libel and slander territory? Were the sisters prepared to deal with the potential fallout from their appearance? The sisters responded with, "Moseby was a powerful figure back then, and we didn't want to open up an unnecessary can of worms, especially since it was likely no one would have believed us," "What kind of evidence do you expect us to have from something that happened when we were kids?" and, "Yes, we're prepared for the aftermath of our appearance if it means potentially bringing Moseby to justice and encouraging others to speak out as well."

That last one was what convinced Helen to have her producers arrange for them to be on the show. One could only do so much with evidence, but the thought of other women out there being scared into silence was heartbreaking. If Helen could shed some light on an issue that let others know it was okay to talk to someone about something so personal, then the taping of today's show would be worth it for that reason alone. Plus, she had been made aware of comedian Cannibal Duress's comments during one of his shows the other night and figured it couldn't be a coincidence. When she found out the sisters had also been at Duress's show, that cinched it. There was something worth exploring here, and she wanted to be the light in the darkness.

She stepped onto the stage of her show's set and looked out at the sea of fans in front of her. So what if she only appealed to certain people? She smiled as she noticed a sprinkling of males mixed in with the mostly female audience; likely accompanying their girlfriends or wives in the hopes it would get them laid later. Probably a gay man or two out there as well, which made her smile even wider. All were welcome on the *Helen* show.

Keeping the seriousness of the topic in mind, she took a deep breath, found the camera the floor director pointed at for her to look into, and began her opening monologue.

"You know, the world never ceases to amaze me, and as much as I try to be the happy-go-lucky type of person whose only ambition and desire is to make everyone feel good, sometimes I need to use my position as a vehicle for some hard-hitting social issues. Today is one of those times. I want you to watch this clip from comedian Cannibal Duress's show last night."

A short clip from Duress's performance was played, where he called Dill Moseby a rapist and urged his victims to speak out.

"It's hard enough being a woman in today's society, but it's made even harder when powerful men who think they're above the law and superior to all of us choose to use their money and influence to attack people, physically, emotionally, or otherwise. With everything that's playing out in the media lately, between the #AndMe movement and the sexual allegations against Hollywood figures that seem to increase in number by the day, it's time for everyone, men and women, to make a stand."

The audience applauded and roared in approval.

"I have on the show today three such women who have decided enough is enough, and I'm honored they reached out to me to help tell their stories. Please help me welcome sisters Brenda, Gigi, and Layanna Lark."

The Lark sisters appeared from backstage to more applause as they each hugged Helen and made their way over to the provided couch to sit down.

"Ladies, thank you so much for being here. I'm happy to help bring attention to the cause and to provide you with a platform for your voices to be heard."

"Thank you for agreeing to have us on, Helen," Brenda said. "It means a lot to us."

"My pleasure. So I understand that wasn't your first time seeing that clip we just played. You three were actually at that show, weren't you?"

"We were," Gigi confirmed. "We were all practically in tears by the end of the night. Duress is such a nice guy. We told one of the people who works for him after the show that we really appreciated him bringing Moseby's crimes to light, because you know, this isn't the first time it's been mentioned, but it's the first time people have started to take it seriously. I don't know if it's because everyone thinks Duress doesn't have a reason to lie or what, but Moseby's image is finally starting to be questioned and we have Duress to thank for that. We got to meet him and expressed our gratitude for him, and he said he was flattered and thanked us for coming to his show. We even got a picture with him."

A picture of the Lark sisters with Duress appeared on screen.

"Very cool," Helen said.

"It was a really great night," Layanna chimed in. "It's always tough to relive hurtful memories from your past, but knowing there's someone out there in your corner makes it a little easier."

"I can imagine," Helen said. "So let's discuss exactly what

happened when each of you met Dill Moseby. You can give as much or as little detail as you'd like, but nothing too graphic. This is still daytime television, after all."

The audience laughed.

"Which of you feels comfortable enough to go first?" Helen asked the sisters.

The three women looked at each other.

"I will," Brenda volunteered.

"Okay, whenever you're ready, dear," Helen encouraged.

Brenda paused a moment to gather her thoughts, took a deep breath, and began.

"We'd been fans of Dill Moseby's for years. The sitcom he starred in was the number-one comedy in the country when we were growing up and our parents took us to see him perform live several times. There was one time we heard he was staying in a hotel close to where we lived during one of his tours, so the three of us actually went there and hung out in the lobby for a bit, hoping we'd get to meet him. After a couple of hours, our gamble paid off and we saw him come out of an elevator and head for the front desk.

"I was the first to call out to him and he turned around and smiled at us. We told him we were big fans and he came up to us and shook our hands, saying it was always nice to meet his fans, especially ones who were as pretty as us. That comment didn't strike us at the time as anything other than a standard compliment. Certainly neither of us were thinking that was his way of hitting on us, especially as teenage girls."

Brenda suddenly stopped talking and tears started forming in her eyes as she envisioned the next part of her narrative.

"Are you all right?" Helen asked her.

Brenda didn't respond, choosing instead to look down at the floor and remain quiet.

"It's okay, Brenda," Gigi consoled her sister. "I'll tell the rest."

Brenda and Gigi hugged each other and Gigi kissed Brenda on the forehead. When Brenda nodded her head in a silent gesture to go on, Gigi nodded back and continued their story.

"He started asking questions to get to know us a bit," Gigi said. "Our ages, where we went to school, if we had any hobbies, boyfriends, what we wanted to do when we got older, things like that. I remember telling him I was interested in becoming a model and his eyes lit up. He said he had a bunch of friends that worked for various modeling agencies and he wanted to discuss my goals in more detail with me. He said we caught him when he was about to head out to dinner, but that maybe the three of us could head up to his room and he would order room service for everyone.

"Of course we loved the idea of being able to spend personal time with one of our idols, so we agreed to go upstairs with him. It was supposed to be a fun conversation over dinner. We had no intention of spending the night because we knew our parents would have killed us."

"We went up in the elevator with him," Layanna cut in, "followed him to his room, and as soon as he unlocked the door to let us in, that's when things got a little weird. He abruptly closed the door, relocked it, and told us to find a place to sit and that he'd be with us in a minute. And he's Dill Moseby, right? So he's obviously staying in this huge suite and the three of us were freaking out at how lucky we were just to be there. We couldn't wait to go to school the next day and brag about our personal visit with one of the most popular comedians of all time."

"He came back from wherever it was he went," Gigi continued, "we all figured he went to the bathroom, and he had these pills in his hand he was suddenly adamant we take. Each of us declined and that seemed to aggravate him a bit, but that irritated look was quickly replaced with his warm, welcoming demeanor again. He ordered food for us and we hung out, laughed, and ate. It didn't occur to us that he might have found a way to plant the pills in the food.

"Once we finished eating, we started to feel light-headed and our first thought was maybe we had gotten food poisoning. It was affecting all of us the same way, so what other explanation could there have been, right? What happened was Moseby had crushed the pills and sprinkled them onto each of our plates when we weren't looking. That sick feeling is the last thing either of us remembers from that day."

"When we woke up the next morning," Layanna continued, "Moseby wasn't even in the room, but we found a note from him thanking us for an enjoyable evening and telling us to keep in touch, with his personal number at the bottom. We were all fully clothed, but we could tell something wasn't right and we had no idea what had happened.

"Our mouths were dry and I found something on my teeth that definitely wasn't food or toothpaste. Brenda and Gigi have their own theories, but I personally believe he had us perform oral sex on him. It explains the odd feeling in each of our mouths and why our clothes didn't appear to be touched or adjusted in any way."

"Oh my god," Helen said. "I'm so sorry to hear what you dealt with, ladies. Brenda, Gigi, what do you think happened after you passed out?"

"I think the sicko fondled us and touched our bodies in various places while he masturbated," Gigi said, looking a little sheepish as she realized the word she just used. "Sorry. Can I say that word on TV? 'Masturbated?'"

"Well, even if you can't, you just said it twice," Helen joked as the audience laughed. "But don't worry. I'm sure if the censors find any problems with it they'll bleep it out."

"I think he had us set up in various poses while we were passed out and took pictures," Brenda said, feeling confident enough to speak again. "And it wouldn't surprise me if he still had them. But whatever he did to us, he couldn't bring himself to face us afterwards. That's why he'd already taken off before we woke up."

The audience began speaking among themselves, speculating about what they just heard. Helen decided it was time to wrap things up and started to steer the taping to a conclusion.

"Well, ladies, again, thank you so much for telling your story here today, and I truly hope this helps get the process rolling in terms of seeing Dill Moseby brought to justice."

"Thank you, Helen," Layanna said. "We're so grateful you let us do this. It means a lot that someone such as yourself took an interest in what we had to say."

Of course it does, Helen thought to herself. *How could you not be grateful? I'm me!*

"Tomorrow's show will be a bit on the lighter side when we welcome the YouTube sensation known as Chin Chin Chin, who only ever speaks that one word," Helen said to the camera. "Tune in as I attempt to teach him the rest of the English language. Thanks for watching!"

Some people's personal lives manage to squeak by under the radar longer than others. For those in the public eye who are scrutinized more than most, it's usually a matter of time before dirty little secrets come to light. Such was the case for Dill Moseby, as the last few days found him splashed all over the media, not for his career, but for his behavior outside the spotlight. Nearly a half-century of doing whatever he pleased, whenever he pleased, a benefit of fame and money he felt he earned from entertaining the masses and serving as a role model for so long, had now led to his fans considering him a monster? The same fans who gave him standing ovations and showered him in adulation and praise? It was ridiculous! As recently as last night he had enjoyed the satisfaction of a job well done, a performance from someone who was still at the top of his game, regardless of his age.

Comedy wasn't as easy as it seemed. One didn't just go up on stage and freestyle or improvise stand-up. Well, maybe some people did, but those people usually sucked at it! Moseby cared enough about both his craft and his audience's experience to spend hours at a time perfecting his sets. And this was the thanks he got for it? Being told he couldn't enjoy the fruits of his labor? What a bunch of ungrateful motherfuckers!

All these thoughts went through his head as he heard footsteps outside his hotel room. Then, when the footsteps stopped, they were replaced with loud pounding on his door. He looked through the door's peephole to see who could possibly have the nerve to bother him in the middle of the afternoon. His eyes went wide as he saw two police officers outside - one male and one female. Damn! Was this really how it was going to end? Did these uniformed cops really think they could drag him from this room and put him in a cell? They didn't have any evidence as far as he was aware. None! What the fuck was happening to this country? The president could blatantly want to have sex with children but he wasn't allowed to drug adults? That was wrong on so many levels.

"Who the hell is it?" Moseby shouted through the door, playing dumb and hoping the officers would leave. "I'm not expecting any visitors and I'm very busy! Go away!"

"This is the police!" the male officer shouted back. "Open the door before we break it down!"

"That's a bit harsh," the female officer said to her partner. "He's a disgusting old man, not an armed criminal."

"It doesn't matter. We need to show force from the start or he won't take us seriously. Just watch me work, Rookie. I'll show you how it's done."

The female officer took a step back, deferring to her cocky colleague.

"The police?" Moseby shouted, continuing to play dumb. "You have no business here! Leave me alone before I call hotel security!"

"The hotel already knows we're here, sir," the female officer said, "and my partner's not known for his patience, so can you please open the door?"

"You've got to learn to drop that nice act, Rookie," the male officer said. "If this was the scene of a burglary, kidnapping, or even a hostage situation, the guy in there would be laughing at you."

"Get out of here right now!" Moseby shouted again. "And don't come back until you have a permit! I've done nothing wrong!"

"I'm going to count to three," the male officer warned. "If you still haven't let us in by then, this door's coming down! One, two..."

Reluctantly, Moseby yielded and opened the door.

"What's going on here, officers?" the comedian asked, dropping the aggressive tone in an effort at playing nice. "I'm going over material for a show later tonight."

"Not anymore!" the male officer said.

"Do you know something I don't?" Moseby asked, feigning confusion.

"You're under arrest, sir," the female officer said, producing handcuffs. "Please turn around so we can put these on you. You have the right to remain silent..."

"You're actually arresting me?" Moseby cried. "For what? What are the charges?"

"Being a complete and total ass-wipe, for one," the male officer snarled.

"Excuse me?" Moseby said.

"That's his way of answering your question," the female officer replied. "What he means to say is, you're under arrest for sexual assault charges."

"You're joking? And whom have I sexually assaulted?"

"A trio of sisters, for one," the male officer said. "But from what we understand, there are plenty of others."

Moseby rolled his eyes, took a deep breath, and decided to cooperate with the cops, turning around so the female officer could put the handcuffs on him. It dawned on him as he was being cuffed that this was real, he was being arrested, and with the #AndMe movement picking up steam and flipping the justice system on its head so that perpetrators were now guilty until being proven innocent rather than the other way around, he had no idea how to get out of this. Fine! So be it! But he was going to make sure another infamous pig was brought into the picture as well.

"Spleensteen!" Moseby blurted out.

"What the fuck?" the female officer replied, surprised at the seemingly random transition of dialogue.

"Carver and Todd Spleensteen!" Moseby continued. "They're a part of this too! Especially Carver! That bastard's just as bad as I am! Ask any actress that's appeared in any of his films! If the legal system awaits me, fine. But I'm not going down unless Spleensteen comes with me! Promise me you'll look into him!"

"You're not exactly in a position to make any kind of demands," the male officer said.

"Please!" Moseby begged. "I'm telling you, you want to arrest someone for sexual assault? The Spleensteen brothers are a goldmine of sexual crimes! Just promise me you'll look into them and I'll go quietly."

"Sounds good to me," the female officer said.

"Fine!" the male officer agreed, sighing and rolling his eyes. "We'll look into it!"

The two officers escorted Moseby away from the hotel, skeptical about the comedian's claims regarding the Spleensteens, but eager to see who else they could fill their quota with, nonetheless.

<u>Chapter 13</u>

JAKE SAT IN FRONT of his computer at home, browsing through the myriad of online news articles about the #AndMe movement, the Hollywood sex scandals, the recent arrest of comedian Dill Moseby, and the investigation that was now being opened into the Spleensteen brothers. He was tired of hearing about all of it. So many accusers with so many allegations had come forward in the last several days, it was crazy! And here he was, now one of those being accused, looking at a career that might be over before it even had a chance to begin. What the hell was Veronica's problem? She knew damn well he hadn't done anything wrong! And poor Courtney! Her only crime was dealing with Veronica's insanity longer than he had. She had probably heard all the claims about the two of them by now and he couldn't help but wonder how she was dealing with it. It's bad enough to become a public name by coming forward with something so personal, but everyone knowing who you are because your so-called best friend chose to spread lies about you for personal gain? That was a new low, even for Veronica.

This is nuts! Jake thought to himself. *I haven't had a single role or job offer since Veronica's ludicrous outburst the other day. A part of me wonders whether or not that's a coincidence.*

He was about to shut down the computer when he noticed a video posted to Veronica's YouTube account a handful of hours ago. Curious as to what she'd been up to since being banned from the apartment, he clicked on it and was treated to quite a scene. The video showed his potentially ex-girlfriend heading a gathering of women at what appeared to be a rally of some sort. Scanning the faces of the attendees, Jake recognized Dick Starter accusers Kelly Swack and Jeanine Harlot, and picket signs that read, "Rape No More," "#AndMe," and, "No Need To Drug If You Want To Fug." Veronica seemed happy and in her element as the center of attention, as she looked at the camera and addressed the assembled crowd.

"It's the twenty-first century and social progress has come to a halt!" Veronica shouted. The gathered women shouted their agreement in unison. "We may be able to vote, we may be able to work and pursue a career of our choice, we may even be able to marry other women, but the moment our male counterparts feel we've accomplished too much, they stand in our way and tell us we can't do anymore unless we tend to their primal urges!"

The women once again shouted their agreement.

"We gather today to tell the men in our lives who have hurt us, enough is enough!" Veronica continued. "We won't stand for this anymore! We're more than just sex objects or baby-making machines! We're human beings, and damn it, we deserve some respect!"

Applause and cheers were heard all around.

"We're sick of the rich and powerful thinking they can do whatever they want just because they have resources! We're through with sitting on the sidelines and keeping quiet while our friends, colleagues, and sisters endure the shame of being used for their bodies and thrown away when they're not wanted anymore! And most importantly, we're through with sex being used as currency for advancement in the work place!

It!...Ends!...Now!”

The cheers and hollers from the gathered women grew even louder.

“Some of you may have already heard of my situation. My world recently shattered all around me when I found out the man I thought I loved forced himself on my best friend. Unfortunately, I heard about this incident after the fact and wasn't around at the time it happened to be able to stop it. I promised I wouldn't use her name, but my friend came to my place earlier in the week and when my boyfriend told her I was out, she decided to stick around until I returned. Why wouldn't she? She's known him for three years. She considered him a friend. She trusted him. And how was that trust repaid? By him taking advantage of the two of them being alone.

“He backed her into a corner of our apartment, wouldn't let her go, and had his way with her. Despite all her protests, pushing him away, and yelling at him to stop, my disgusting pig of a boyfriend used my best friend to grunt his way to climax. What if the roles were reversed? What if we had a gay roommate who wouldn't keep his hands off him no matter how many times he said no, who was eager to thrust into him every time he bent over, even if it was only mockingly? Rest assured if men were treated half as bad as they treated us, there would be arrests, litigation, and rules, rules, rules, every which way but loose! And who exactly is this man my best friend no longer feels comfortable around, you may ask? The incomparable Jake Asworth!”

The women started chattering among themselves, trying to determine whether or not they've heard that name before.

“You may recognize that name from his cheap attempts at acting. Jake has been a part of pizza commercials, a spokesman for a local business, and more recently, was supposed to have been a part of R&B singer M. Belly's latest music video. But just as his career might have developed into something to be proud of, he ruined it by not only cheating on me, but raping a young lady who thought he was a friend. Let this be a lesson to those who seek to undermine us! We won't be ignored! We won't be intimidated! And just when you think you've gotten away with it, we'll be there to hold you accountable for your actions! Thank you!”

Veronica ended her speech and went to mingle with the crowd, taking in all the praise and adulation. She'd finally done it! She was a voice of the people, and nothing was going to take that away from her.

Jake, meanwhile, sat in his apartment, staring at his computer screen in shock at what he'd just watched.

"Well, that explains my lack of job offers lately," he said aloud to himself. "If that video's gone viral, I'm screwed. What's your endgame, Veronica? You really think you can further your own reputation by tarnishing mine?"

He opened up a web cam program, preparing to record a video of his own.

"Time to attempt some damage control."

He pressed record and began to speak.

"Hi! Jake Asworth here. I have a feeling that thanks to a certain someone, if you didn't know who I was before, you probably do now. I know with all of the other allegations floating around out there at the moment, everyone who watches this will likely take this statement with a grain of salt, but I want to go on record as saying this incident where I apparently forced myself on my girlfriend's best friend never happened. I know a rebuttal like this is to be expected. If someone does something like that, they're not just going to come out and admit it, right? That would only further taint their reputation. But in my case, it's true. It never happened.

"I hope she doesn't hate me too much for publicly revealing her identity, but the friend's name in question is Courtney Coccyx, and I've known her for as long as Veronica and I have been dating. Anyone who happens to run into her can ask her about this. It simply isn't true. Veronica and I are both aspiring actors and she's obviously jealous of casting directors taking more interest in me for their projects than her. I'm not going to sit here and ramble on and on. All I can do at this point is defend myself and hope the truth prevails."

Jake stopped recording and immediately proceeded to upload the video to his own YouTube channel and social media profiles, hoping it would make a dent in planting the seeds of doubt in people and start to clear his name.

Meanwhile, Veronica continued to mingle with the women who had shown up at her rally, basking in the attention and thoroughly enjoying her new role as poster child, when she was approached by Kelly Swack and Jeanine Harlot. Kelly and Jeanine were the ones who had reached out to her to give voice to their cause after the M. Belly music video fiasco, and they couldn't have been happier when she agreed to be their mascot. Former assistants to Hollywood powerhouses, Cheyenne Sofarro and Erica Sudds, were on hand supporting the rally too, as well as aspiring actress Felicia Donner.

"Great speech, Veronica!" Kelly greeted her new friend. "Thank you so much for doing this!"

"Totally!" Jeanine agreed. "I thought all of our words were going to continue to fall on deaf ears, but then Kelly told me about you and here we are."

"Thanks, ladies! Happy to help!" Veronica said. "I still can't believe that the situation during the M. Belly shoot made me so popular so fast. All I did was mention I was uncomfortable working with my boyfriend and it's been nothing but interview requests and media coverage ever since."

"I just knew when we heard about you that you'd be perfect to act as the face of this whole thing!" Kelly gushed. "Nobody started taking us seriously until you came along!"

"And I'm pretty sure your appearances single-handedly led to the arrests of Dill Moseby and the Spleensteens," Jeanine said.

"I'm flattered you think I had so much to do with it," Veronica told them, "but it was actually the sisters who were on *Helen* that led to Moseby's arrest, and I heard of all people, Moseby himself was the one who ratted out the Spleensteens."

"The Spleensteens are such pigs!" Felicia declared. "I've never been happier to see two people face public humiliation than I was when I saw their faces as they were led off their studio lot in handcuffs!"

"I know what you mean," Erica agreed. "Seachest has managed to maintain his career, but at least now there are seeds of doubt planted in the public's psyche, and that's immensely satisfying."

"Triple T's image doesn't seem to have been hurt too much either," Cheyenne chimed in. "I'll never understand how people can constantly get away with these things. I'm not asking for the man to be publicly lynched, I just want him to admit he's done wrong and apologize, but I guess that's too much to ask."

"Dick Starer's career with the Sidestreet Dudes doesn't seem to have been impacted much either," Kelly said, putting an arm around Veronica. "But at least we have our bulldog, right, ladies?"

Everyone cheered in agreement.

"Whatever convictions we don't see today, we can fight to see tomorrow! Veronica has shown us that whatever we can't accomplish alone, we can accomplish together! We are women, hear us roar!"

The gathered ladies cheered and hollered again, enjoying themselves until a familiar voice broke in.

"That's right! Cheer for your champion! Who cares if she's a liar?"

Everyone started looking around to see where the voice came from and a look of shame crossed Veronica's face when she recognized her friend, Courtney.

"A liar? What are you talking about?" Jeanine asked, turning to Veronica. "Veronica, who is this?"

"Apparently, I'm the best friend who doubles as a convenient rape victim!" Courtney shouted, while Veronica remained silent.

"You're the one her boyfriend took advantage of?" Kelly asked. "Oh, honey, I'm so sorry!"

Kelly went to hug Courtney but was brushed off.

"No, you don't understand," Courtney said. "Veronica has been lying to you. Jake and I have never had sex, forceful or otherwise. We're friends. He would never do that to me."

"Oh, she's in denial," Jeanine said, gesturing for her to join their group. "It's okay, hon. You're among friends now. Come over here and let us comfort you."

"How dense are you people?" Courtney snapped. "I haven't been raped by anybody! Veronica made the whole thing up!"

All eyes were once more on Veronica.

"Is that true?" Felicia asked.

Veronica didn't answer.

"Damn it, Veronica, tell them!" Courtney snarled. "You wanted your own fifteen minutes of fame, so you used everything that's been going on lately to your advantage!"

"Why would you do that?" Cheyenne asked, seemingly hurt. "We trusted you!"

"Come on, Veronica, be honest with us," Erica said. "Is your friend here telling the truth?"

Veronica looked down at the ground, choosing not to face anybody, as she sheepishly answered.

"Yes," she quietly replied.

"I can't believe this!" Kelly shouted.

"How could you?" Jeanine asked.

"Do you have any idea how serious those allegations are?" Felicia chimed in.

"Hey, come on!" Veronica spoke up, getting defensive. "You were just heaping praise onto me and now I'm a villain? My telling a little white lie doesn't change the good I've done for you! Look around! See all these people? They're just like you! They're here to support you! Look at those news vans! Wait a minute. News vans? Fuck!"

Two news vans, one from PBN and one from Alpha Beta, were just pulling up to the park where the rally was taking place, as two reporters from each network approached with their cameramen in tow.

"Veronica Scarlett! Can we have a word?" The PBN reporter asked.

"I'd like to ask you a few questions as well, Miss Scarlett!" echoed the Alpha Beta reporter.

"Forget it! You're wasting your time! All of this is a lie!" Courtney told them.

“Interesting. Now we really need to talk,” the PBN reporter said.

“Indeed,” the Alpha Beta reporter agreed.

“Listen, I'm not perfect, okay?” Veronica said, choosing to stay on the defensive. “I saw an opportunity and I took advantage of it. Am I proud of what I did? No! I actually felt a little guilty when Jake looked at me with hurt in his eyes after I accused him of abusing my friend. But people are paying attention to all of you now! They're finally starting to take you seriously! Isn't that what everybody wanted?”

“It was never about them, Veronica!” Courtney said. “It was about you! You, being in the spotlight, no matter the reason. You, hoping to blacklist Jake so more projects would consider you for their roles. As long as we've been friends, sometimes I forget how much of an egomaniac you are!”

“Tell us what she's talking about, Miss Scarlett!” said the PBN reporter.

“How long did it take you to plan this deception?” asked the Alpha Beta reporter.

“Talk to them,” Veronica said, gesturing to the girls around her. “They're the real story. They're your victims. I'm not a victim of anything other than my ego. I'm sorry.”

Veronica walked away from the scene, leaving everyone behind. The two reporters started asking questions of the rest of the girls while those who remained continued to walk around holding their picket signs.

There were so many names in the crowded late-night television landscape that the hosts were always competing with each other, doing their best to determine what guests and musical acts would attract the highest amount of viewers to justify calling themselves the King of Late-Night. Some navigated the waters better than others, and Timmy Thimble was one of them. Having found success as a talk show host and comic, *Timmy Thimble Live!* was currently celebrating its eighteenth season on the air, and while most television personalities would claim their show's popularity was all their doing, Thimble knew his writers, his production crew, and most importantly, his fans, were what kept the show relevant and in good standing with the network throughout the years.

But as humble and modest as he was, he knew he played a pivotal role in his show's success as well. He contributed to all the segments, wrote his own opening monologues, and personally hand-picked all the guests who appeared. Tonight's show was no different. With all the scandals emerging out of Hollywood lately and all the young ladies coming forward claiming they had personal experiences with a star's genitalia, Thimble knew he wanted to address all the controversies during the taping. Like all good comedians, though, he didn't want to approach the topic with too heavy of a hand. The agreed-upon formula for people in his position seemed to be "tragedy plus time equals comedy", and while the timing of the recent tragedies was too, well, recent, he also knew that tackling the subject from a certain angle could result in big laughs and a very successful episode. So what had he decided to do? Prepare a monologue and an entire show around one of the #AndMe movement's biggest antagonists, of course!

"So, it turns out comedian Dill Moseby has finally been arrested," Thimble said to his audience as the show began. "And apparently, he ratted out the Spleensteen brothers so he wouldn't have to be the only one to go to jail."

The audience laughed.

"It's crazy to think those guys have gotten away with everything they're being accused of for so many years! When just a couple of women come out and tell a story like that, everyone thinks they're after money. But when multiple women all start saying the same thing having never met each other before, that's admittedly a little harder to overlook. Then there's this Veronica Scarlett chick who seemingly came out of nowhere! She was starting to become somewhat of a poster child for this whole thing until the friend she was talking about came forward herself and called her out for lying. How crazy is that?

"Here you have a young lady who's arguably a big reason why a lot of these other women started being taken seriously, and then just when you're thinking everything makes sense, you're questioning everything all over again. This is quite possibly the most serious, and at the same time, ridiculous, media circus in recent memory.

"But that's enough waxing poetic. We've got a great show tonight! M. Belly is here! And we all know he's obviously not involved in any scandals!"

The audience laughed once more, knowing exactly the kind of person M. Belly was, as Thimble headed behind his desk on the set.

This is why I became a comedian, Thimble thought to himself. *I can shove recent events in people's faces and good or bad, they love me for it. Who could ask for anything better?*

Chapter 14

THE JUSTICES OF THE Supreme Court knew the task ahead of them could potentially result in something historic. Their job on this day was to gather and debate the merits of the recently proposed Good to Go Law. Some saw the genius behind it while others wondered how their counterparts could be so dense. The concept of sex with whomever you wanted, whenever you wanted, seemed great in theory, but, as all things related to sex go, in practice, the logistics behind it proved much more complicated. The ramifications weren't as black and white as they may have seemed.

Even if the Court decided to uphold the bill today, questions would remain. How would you define a "minor," or an "adult?" Regardless of the legality, there were ethical and moral considerations as well. How would one know if their partner was "too young?" Or, with the age of consent completely abolished, would there be such a thing as "too young" anymore? How would abortion play into this? Surely, with adult males being given the green light to sleep with young females of any age, the question would inevitably be asked, what was the minimal acceptable age for girls to give birth and become parents? All these issues and more were on the minds of each of the Justices as they settled into their seats to discuss this potential new law.

"Okay, people, it's up to us," Justice One said. "We can make or break this bill. As much as I support the president's pursuit of the...finer things in life, my gut instinct is to kill it. What say the rest of you?"

"I'm not sure," said Justice Two. "There would definitely be advantages to this bill passing."

"Such as?" Justice Three asked.

"We all know how overfull our jails are, right?" Justice Two continued. "I'm completely making this statistic up, but let's say for argument's sake roughly half of the people we incarcerate are doing time for possession of drugs or sexual crimes, which are technically considered lesser offenses in the grand scheme of things. If we can at least stop filling cells with people who are only as dangerous as they are horny, we can free up a lot more space in those facilities and stop wasting taxpayers' money on housing those clowns."

Justice Three wasn't buying it.

"So you're saying you want to not only allow child molesters to get away with any and all future behavior, but you want to go a step further and release those who have already been sentenced?"

"I'll put it to you this way," Justice Two said. "Say we use our power to kill this thing and life goes on as it always has. Everyone sitting in this room knows how impulsive our president is. Who wants to be the one to watch him get carted away in handcuffs because it gets to a point where he can no longer control his lustful desires?"

They all looked around the room to get a feel of each other's thoughts. Nobody seemed to want to imagine a scenario in which their president was arrested for anything.

"That's what I thought," Justice Two said, resting his case.

"Come off it!" Justice One cried. "Not wanting to see the president get arrested isn't a good enough reason to allow this thing to pass! After everything he's already been through - the investigations, the sexual allegations that already exist, the evidence that both his business and political practices are shady as fuck - he's come out of everything unscathed. We tell him he's above the law daily by choosing to do nothing more than give him a slap on the wrist. Does anyone think it's really going to matter at this point if we say, 'Sorry, sir, no fucking kids'?

"The president's gonna do what the president's gonna do, no matter what. Kill this bill and allow children to walk around their neighborhoods without a source of contraception in their back pockets! That's where I stand on this, and nobody's going to get me to change my mind!"

"What about your girlfriend?" Justice Four asked.

"What about her?" Justice One replied, defensively.

"Nothing. I would just think you'd benefit from this bill. She's a lot younger than you, isn't she?"

"She's nineteen, which means she's legal, thank you very much!" Justice One said. "Can we focus less on my personal life and more on the topic at hand, please?"

"Does anyone else have anything important to add, or are we putting this puppy to bed?" Justice Three asked.

"I'm ready to vote if the rest of you are," Justice Four replied. "I think regardless of our biases, we all know what the right thing to do is."

All the Justices looked at each other and nodded, as if in silent agreement. The modern-day world was a crazy place, all right, but they had the power to make it a little less crazy, and that's what they decided to do.

Jake was lying in bed, emotionally drained after everything that had happened, and trying to take an afternoon nap, when he heard a knock on his front door.

"Go away!" he shouted, not wanting to get up.

"Jake, open the door!" Veronica called out. "I want to talk to you!"

That woman's got some nerve! Jake thought to himself. *After everything she's said and done, she thinks she can just waltz back here like nothing happened? I don't think so!*

"We have nothing to talk about, Veronica!" he called back to her.

"You're mad at me. I get that. But can you at least let me apologize?"

"Why don't you apologize to Courtney? If she's still willing to talk to you afterwards, then maybe, maybe, I'll consider considering the same."

"Veronica and I have already spoken, Jake," came Courtney's voice. "Now we're here to speak to you."

How do you like that? Veronica and Courtney have become so co-dependent on each other they've somehow managed to put this crazy episode behind them. Well, good for them! That doesn't mean I have to follow suit!

Just because he was curious to see what Courtney had to say after playing the fictional victim to his fictional rapist, he got out of bed and opened the door.

"I'm surprised you don't hate her as much as I do right now, Court," Jake said. "She lied about both of us, you know."

"Trust me," Courtney said, giving Veronica the stink-eye, "I know."

Jake let Courtney and Veronica into his home and closed the door.

"Okay, Veronica, you've got my attention," Jake said. "But you should know that if your plan is to play the pity card, it's not going to work. Neither is the two of you ganging up on me going to convince me to give Veronica another chance."

"I'm personally not here to convince you of anything, Jake," Courtney said. "I just want you to know that Veronica still loves you, still cares about you, and quite frankly, she doesn't have anywhere else to go."

"Okay. Why can't she tell me all of that?"

"Fine. I still love you, I still care about you, and quite frankly, I have nowhere else to go," Veronica echoed her friend. "Satisfied?"

"Not even remotely!"

"Look, you know me. You know that I'm a person very much driven by my id. I've always been that way and I'll always be that way. I got jealous of not being as successful in my career as you've been in yours, and that led me to do something very impulsive and incredibly stupid. Admittedly, I can't say I'll never do something like that again, because I'd be lying to you and that's not what I want to do right now, but I can say I'll try to be a little bit better about controlling my impulses."

"Try to be better about controlling your impulses?" Jake shouted. "Do you understand how serious the lies are you told about Courtney and me? You made her out to be a victim and me a sexual predator! Then you have the audacity to come back here, tell me you can't promise it won't happen again, but you still want to be a part of my life? I think some therapy is an order before I can even think about wanting to be around you again!"

"That's fair. But you know, Courtney's bi."

"Veronica!" Courtney cried. "What does that have to do with anything?"

"Because if I get lonely while waiting for Jake to take me back, maybe we can hook up, eh?" Veronica said, putting an arm around her friend and laughing.

"I know you're joking," Courtney said, taking Veronica's hand off, "but now's really not the time."

"See? She can't take anything seriously! Ever!" Jake said. "I've dealt with your craziness for long enough, and I think right now you've really got to..."

Veronica cut Jake off by kissing him. He stood there, stunned at first, as if processing what just happened. Finally, he gave in to his own primal urges, took his girlfriend into his arms, and kissed her back, leading to a full-fledged make-out session while Courtney watched them, smiling at their unofficial reconciliation.

The president was sitting behind his desk, doing his best to look busy when he really had nothing important going on. His good mood from earlier in the week went sour after there wound up being enough riots from his Good to Go bill for the Supreme Court to intervene and debate the case. Last he had heard, they were about to make their final decision, but he didn't know what that was yet. Just as he was considering putting his feet on the desk and taking another nap, his son-in-law, Ferret Bushner, and press secretary, Tara Blanders, entered the room.

"Sir, I'm afraid we have some news for you," Tara said to her boss.

"Afraid? That means it's bad news?"

"Very perceptive, sir," Ferret said.

Suddenly, the president, being the president, went off on a wild tangent that had nothing to do with the topic of conversation.

"I've been watching reruns of that series, *The Big Bang Theory.* Either of you ever see that show?"

Ferret and Tara looked at each other, not sure how to respond.

"Every now and then, perhaps," Ferret finally replied.

"Well, there's this character on the show, Sheldon, he starts off as not really understanding what people around him are saying. But in later episodes, he becomes more aware of things like sarcasm, when people treat him unfairly, and stuff like that. I'm trying to be more like him."

"Always good to have goals, sir," Ferret said to his father-in-law.

"I agree. So, about this news you have for me. Where's Yolanda? Why didn't she want to tell me this news?"

"Your daughter's busy tending to matters related to her clothing line, sir," Tara said.

"That's a shame," the president said, sounding disappointed. "I haven't seen her all day."

"Anyway," Tara continued, pretending she hadn't been interrupted, "the Supreme Court just prevented the Good to Go Law from passing on moral grounds. They believe that children are just too young to make certain decisions, including those of a sexual nature, and that's why they've decided to keep the age of consent intact."

"What?" The president shouted, pounding on his desk in anger. "That's outrageous! Fake news!"

"I'm afraid it's very much real news, sir," Ferret said.

"Geez! Nobody will let me do anything around here! Those damn

Democrats are always conspiring against me!"

"Actually, the Supreme Court that exists right now is the most conservative-leaning one we've had for quite some time," Ferret corrected the president.

Tara and the president then shared a look with each other, surprised Ferret could claim a stake in knowing such information.

"Fine! So I don't get to sleep with Olivia. Why did it take two of you to tell me that?"

"Mr. Bushner here was afraid to tell you by himself," Tara taunted the man sitting to her right.

"Tara! Let the cat out of the bag, much?"

"Hey, you want to be a coward, I'll paint you as one!"

"Okay, well, thanks for stopping by," the president said, cutting off their argument. "If you don't mind, I'd really like to get back to just sitting here."

"There is actually one more thing you should know, sir," Ferret said.

"So spit it out!"

"Our intelligence community has just received word that Iran has taken down an American drone, and, well, they're apparently bragging about it to anyone who will listen."

If Ferret and Tara thought the president was mad at the news of his failed bill, they were about to witness a whole new level of rage, as he got up with a furious look on his face and spoke in a tone that indicated he wanted blood.

"What? That is un-fucking-acceptable! I'll teach them to mess with our expensive toys! Tara, go put together a press conference and announce to the world our intention to seek vengeance! Ferret, I'm still not quite sure what it is you usually do, but go do it! I've got to make a call to Vladdy and complain about this!"

The president got up and stormed out of the room.

"Vladdy?" Ferret said to Tara. "You don't think he means..."

"I'd rather not know. What I don't know, I don't have to lie about."

"At least he changed gears quickly enough. Now he's got

something else to focus on other than the bill he was touting as his political legacy."

"Just another day at the White House, huh?" Tara said. "With Mr. Amazing always shifting from one topic to the next, depending on what concerns his ego the most."

"You think he'll ever get a handle on this president thing?"

"I very much doubt it."

Ferret and Tara suddenly heard the president yelling and screaming down the hall about the downed drone to everyone he passed by.

"We lost one of our drones!" the president cried. "Gone, just like that! How could they do this to us? They'll pay! We'll get them all! Mark my words, they will pay!"

The two shook their heads and hurried out of the room, duty-bound to calm him down. Just another day at the White House, indeed.

ABOUT THE AUTHOR

Jerry Belitch is a comedy writer, stand-up comedian, and indie film director/producer. His other novels include the political satire *Population: One*, and *Fifty Ways to Slay*, a parody of the popular romance trilogy of novels. He lives in Southern California. Visit his website at www.JerryBelitch.com to stay up to date on his latest projects.

* 9 7 9 8 2 1 8 3 1 5 6 1 0 *